W9-AGV-649

BRANCH

		DATE DUE		

WHILE NO ONE WAS WATCHING

WHILE NO ONE
WAS WATCHING

JANE LESLIE CONLY

Henry Holt and Company
New York

Henry Holt and Company, Inc., *Publishers since 1866*
115 West 18th Street, New York, New York 10011

Henry Holt is a registered trademark of Henry Holt and Company, Inc.

Published in Canada by Fitzhenry & Whiteside Ltd.,
195 Allstate Parkway, Markham, Ontario L3R 4T8.

Library of Congress Cataloging-in-Publication Data
Conly, Jane Leslie. While no one was watching / Jane Leslie Conly.
p.   cm.
Summary: When two brothers steal a rabbit from a backyard in the rich part of town,
the incident brings about their collision with other children from a background
very different from their own. [1. City and town life—Fiction. 2. Brothers—Fiction.
3. Rabbits—Fiction.] I. Title. PZ7.C761846Wh   1998   [Fic]—dc21   97-48718

ISBN 0-8050-3934-1   First Edition—1998
Designed by Meredith Baldwin

Printed in the United States of America on acid-free paper. ∞
10 9 8 7 6 5 4 3 2 1

To Megan Sheridan, who gave me the idea
of the Children's Police, and to Sophie,
who is just a little bit like Angela

WHILE NO ONE WAS WATCHING

ONE

They found the yard while Wayne was collecting bicycles. Frankie followed his brother Earl just like he was supposed to, and Earl followed Wayne, who was his cousin, and older. Sometimes Wayne let Earl ride a bike, if they found more than one. Then Frankie would run alongside, saying, "Let me have a turn!" Wayne never gave him a turn, because Frankie didn't have good balance for his age, so he hadn't learned to ride a two-wheeler. He could ride a Big-Wheels, but Wayne never got Big-Wheels, even though Frankie asked him to. All Wayne answered was, "If you don't do what I say, Fat Frankie, you'll have to stay home by yourself."

Frankie didn't like staying in the house by himself, and the big boys weren't supposed to leave him there either, but they sometimes did. They said Frankie couldn't run fast enough to keep up, and that he whined like a baby, like Angela. He tried not to whine, but sometimes he couldn't help it. They walked so far, and they forgot about eating lunch and going to the bathroom and resting. Once Frankie made the mistake of saying he wished kindergarten went through the summer. Wayne and Earl laughed and said he was a dork. But Frankie couldn't help remembering the big round clock on the classroom wall. It never broke, day after day, and when the hands were in a certain place they had snack, and later, lunch, and naptime. Mrs. Chase played music during naptime. Frankie had heard there would be no music in first grade.

"Frankie, hurry!" Earl said over his shoulder. "And shut up!" Frankie sighed. He liked to sing, but he couldn't rush and sing at the same time. And the big boys were always rushing. They had a thousand places to go.

The summer had started better. They had stayed near Aunt Lula's, hanging with other kids in front of Mr. Kim's store. Frankie had sat on the steps of Lula's brick rowhouse. Lula said to watch out for trouble, and he tried to, but he wasn't always sure what trouble looked like. Once he'd seen a man and woman arguing in front of their car; the man had pulled a gun out of his coat pocket. Another day the police had come around the corner with their sirens blaring. He'd seen a dog pee on Lula's flowers right in front of the house, while the woman who held the leash stood there watching. Earl had been in the store getting a pack of gum, but Frankie told him about it later. Earl rolled his eyes. "That's nothing, Fat Frankie." he explained. "A gun is trouble. A dog peeing is nothing." Frankie decided to tell Lula anyway. But she was tired when she got home from her job at the laundry. She drank beer while she made supper, and afterwards she fell asleep at the table. Then Frankie and Earl and their six-year-old sister Angela talked. Angela was a liar.

"Lula said I can have the rest of the mashed potatoes 'cause I went on a trip today," she announced.

Frankie thought for once she might be telling the truth. "Where did you go?"

"To Hollywood." Angela reached for the bowl. "I bought a box of sugar. Then I took the train back to daycamp. Miss Cathy was so glad to see me she gave me a gold medal."

"You can't have all those potatoes," Earl said. "You'll get fat, too."

"I will not! Miss Cathy says I look just like a girl on TV."

"Hulk Hogan's sister, maybe." Earl took the bowl back. He gave a spoonful of potatoes to Angela and one to himself.

"I'm hungry," Frankie whined.

"There's some on your plate already."

Frankie ate as fast as he could, so there'd be potatoes left in the bowl when his were gone. The potato in his mouth was so packed he couldn't swallow. He took a drink of milk to loosen it up, but there wasn't room for the milk and most of it ran down his chin. "Daddy ubed da make graby," he said.

Angela stared at him. "Frankie can speak French," she told Earl.

"Frankie can't speak French. He's got so much food in his mouth he can't talk at all."

Frankie swallowed three times. "Daddy used to make gravy," he said.

"Daddy's in Honolulu." That was Angela.

"He is not. He's on the Eastern Shore, picking vegetables. Beth-ann saw him there, didn't she, Earl?"

Earl shrugged. Frankie saw he'd learned a trick from Wayne. He could close his face the way you pulled the shade down on a window. Then there was just his stringy red hair and a white blank like a wall underneath it. "I don't know," he said.

"She did see him! And we've got his letters—one every Saturday. You had them under your pillow."

Earl shrugged again. Lula stirred in her sleep. Frankie wondered if she would wake up and ask about Wayne. If she asked, he was supposed to lie, because she didn't want them playing with Wayne, even though he was her own son. He lived with his father now, and Lula claimed she didn't want to know where he went or what he did. Wayne didn't want her to know, either. He had threatened Frankie, saying, "If you tell, I'll cut your throat." Frankie could imagine how much it would hurt to have your throat cut. Wayne might do it, too, if he told. Wayne had killed a cat with his bare hands. Even Earl was afraid of Wayne, and Earl was eleven.

"Come on, Frankie," Earl called. "You have to keep up."

"I'm trying." Frankie walked a little faster. They had passed Grover Park and crossed the boulevard. So far Wayne hadn't found any bikes. But he didn't seem to be looking hard, not yet. That morning he'd said he had a new place to look.

Frankie sighed. There was a new place last week, too, and it had also been a long walk, and once they'd arrived, the people hadn't been friendly. It was a college, Wayne said, and there were loads of bikes, but almost all of them belonged to someone, because they were locked up. And while they were looking around, some people from the college asked what they were doing, so they had to leave. Wayne was mad. The whole trip had been a waste of time.

"Maybe if you went at night," Earl said thoughtfully.

"Those bikes aren't there at night. They take them home. You don't know anything," Wayne said. Earl shrugged. His face went blank. "Hurry up, Fat Frankie," he said.

"I'm right here!" Frankie shouted.

But Friday they left Frankie home because he was so slow. He had to spend the day watching TV and coloring in a *He-Man Coloring Book*. The only thing he could find to eat was bread and peanut butter. He was so bored and lonely it was awful. He wished he could go to Miss Cathy's daycamp, like Angela, but Lula said now that he was seven, going into first grade, he was big enough to stay with Earl. Monday he promised to walk really fast. Wayne shook his head, but Frankie begged, and even Earl said, "Come on, man," until finally Wayne said it was okay.

The new place was also across the boulevard, but in

the other direction. They passed a drugstore on the way. Frankie wanted to go in and look at the candy, but the older boys said no. Frankie knew if it was him and Earl, Earl would have done it, because Earl liked to look at the candy too. Sometimes Lula gave them a dollar to split, and they bought candy at Mr. Kim's. But the drugstore had a whole aisle filled with candy.

"Frankie!"

"Here I come!" He hurried from the drugstore window. "Are we almost there?"

"Almost." Wayne stopped and looked around. His long thin nose reminded Frankie of a rat. "It's this way."

They walked up a steep hill. Wayne didn't slow down, but Frankie couldn't help slowing down. They passed a dry cleaner and a gas station. At the top of the hill was a stone wall with an arched doorway. Inside, the houses were bigger, and there were trees almost as big as the ones in the park. And there was grass like the park, only nicer, because alongside the grass were lots of flowers. It didn't look like any dogs had been peeing on them, either.

"Not that house," Wayne murmured. "There's a car in the driveway. And not that one. The next one."

"This one?" Earl's voice was higher than usual.

"Yeah."

They went around the side and crouched behind the hedge. You could see through into the backyard.

"I thought so," Wayne said. "See?"

Frankie stared. There were two bikes on the grass. Next to them was a wooden swing set with two swings, a slide, and a ladder.

"There's no one home," Earl said. "No cars out front, and no lights on."

"They could be there," Wayne said, scowling. "You can't be sure from that."

"I want to swing," Frankie said. Earl started to say no, but Wayne shushed him.

"You can swing if you're quiet," he told Frankie. "If someone comes, tell them you're visiting your uncle down the street."

"Okay." Frankie would tell them anything if he could swing. He liked pushing off and flying back and forth, back and forth. Wayne nodded: Go ahead.

The yard was full of neat stuff: a hammock and a book and a little wooden house with a wire fence around it. There was a ball and some comics and someone's sweatshirt just lying on the grass like no-body would come along and take them. But I'll swing first, Frankie told himself. He sat down and pushed off. The park swings were rubber, but the wood seat on this one worked just as well. He pushed and stretched. The cool, shady yard bathed his sticky face. Wayne and Earl watched from behind the hedge. Frankie felt so good he started singing a song he'd learned from Mr. Tiptop, "Jesus Loves Me," but before he got to the second verse, a small brown rabbit hopped out of the wooden house and up to the fence. It stood on its hind legs and stared at Frankie.

"Hey!" Frankie had seen a rabbit before, when he was little. He had been with Daddy, near the baseball diamond in Grover Park. The little animal was eating, but when it saw them it froze. A minute later it kicked up its heels and ran away. "Let's catch it!" Frankie'd shouted, but Daddy only laughed. "He'd leave us in the dust, Frankie boy," he'd said, cupping his large hand around Frankie's neck. "We're slowpokes."

"I'm not!"

But Daddy had smiled and shaken his head. "Rabbits are wild, son."

"I'm wild, too!" Frankie yelled, and Daddy chased him up the block and around the corner to the bus stop.

Now Frankie looked over his shoulder to show Earl

and Wayne. But they were wheeling the bikes through a hole in the hedge. Frankie turned back and stuck his fingers through the wire. The rabbit sniffed them carefully. Then it rubbed against them. Its brown ears were edged in black, and its fur was softer than anything Frankie had ever felt.

"You're a girl, aren't you? Like Beth-ann . . ."

The rabbit stared.

"Beth-ann's daddy's girlfriend. She let us blow bubbles in her yard and she bought us pop and french fries. We could sit in her lap whenever we wanted to." Frankie paused. Beth-ann was working on the Eastern Shore too. He hadn't known he missed her so much until right now. Beth-ann was soft too—soft and pretty. He missed her blond hair and silky blouses and high-heeled shoes.

"Fat Frankie!" Wayne and Earl were back. "Let's go!"

"Not yet." Frankie wanted them to feel the rabbit, so they could see how soft she was, but Wayne grabbed his arm.

"We got to get out of here."

"*Not yet!*" Frankie could feel what Earl and Angela called his "stubborns" coming up inside him. He wrapped all ten fingers through the wire mesh and dug his heels into the yard.

Earl told Wayne, "If you don't turn him loose, he'll holler."

Wayne cursed.

Earl said, "Frankie, what is it?"

"I want . . ." Frankie stopped. All at once he knew he couldn't have what he wanted: for Daddy and Beth-ann to be here, and for Earl to be nice like he used to. He'd come all this way and they wouldn't even let him ride the bikes, he knew suddenly. They would ride off and leave him to run behind them. "I want . . ." Something soft touched his fingers. "I want the rabbit."

Wayne cursed again. He flung open the cage door and reached inside. The rabbit hissed and dodged. For an awful second Frankie thought Wayne was going to kill it and he started to howl, but Earl put his hand over Frankie's mouth. Wayne snatched the sweatshirt from the ground and threw it over the rabbit. He picked it up and hit it hard. It stopped moving. He handed the bundle to Frankie.

"It's dead," Frankie moaned, but then he felt a little twitch under the fabric.

"You better keep up, Frankie," Earl said. "If you don't keep up, I'm taking it away."

They ran for the bikes. Wayne and Earl rode them out, but Earl's legs were too short, so he had to balance over the pedals instead of sitting down. Frankie ran behind them till they were out of sight. Then he stopped running. He could feel something moving under his arm.

He walked through the arch in the wall and down the hill. There was Grover Park and the drugstore. "We're going to Lula's," he told the rabbit. "We're living there till Daddy comes back. Then we'll get our own house, like before."

The bundle twitched.

"Don't worry," Frankie told it. "We're almost there."

TWO

Earl was worried. He had a knot in his stomach that felt like a hardball. Not only that, but Frankie hadn't come home. Who knows where he'd gone? Any other kid would have remembered the park and the boulevard and the drugstore, but Frankie was in a world of his own. And he had the sweatshirt. What if somebody asked him what was in it? Frankie would probably say, "It's a rabbit. We took it out of somebody's yard."

Earl groaned. A chill passed over him, with the pain of stomachache right behind it. He'd better look for Frankie, before someone else found him first.

He went out to the alley and began to run. His stomach hurt, but he knew from experience that running would help the pain. He focused on breathing: in and out, in and out, to the rhythm of his strides. Sometimes he felt he could run forever. Years ago one of his teachers, Mr. Briggs, noticed how fast he was: "They'll want to get their hands on you to run cross-country, Earl." But there was no track until you got to high school, and high school was a long way off.

"Frankie!" he called. His voice echoed off the backs of the rowhouses. The tiny yards he passed were crammed with furniture: picnic tables, hanging lights, metal swing sets. Dogs strained at their chains, barking and snapping. "Frankie," he called. "Fat Frankie— where *are* you?"

He ran on, feeling the knot in his stomach loosen. He focused on the center line of the concrete alley as if it were a tightrope. He imagined a finish line, far ahead, and he broke the tape, raising his arms in victory. People came to shake his hand, but out of habit he made sure those from the good side of the tightrope touched him first: Daddy and Beth-ann, Frankie and Angela, Mr. Briggs, his old friends Mikey and Fernando. These were the people who'd believed in him all along, who wanted him to do well and were kind to him when he did, and sometimes even when he didn't. But lately the good side had lost ground. Mikey had moved to Emmitsburg, and Fernando joined the Born-Again Church that met in the old movie theater. Sometimes he was so goody-good it made the other kids sick. Then Daddy got laid off. They lost their house and moved in with Beth-ann. But it turned out her landlord didn't want kids there, and they didn't have the money to get another place. After that Daddy heard about work on a farm on the Eastern Shore. The pay was okay, but there was only a single room to stay in, so he planned to come back as soon as he'd saved a down payment. In the meantime his sister Lula wanted the kids with her.

"Lula's good-hearted, but she falls apart when things get rough," Earl had overheard him say.

"It's just a few months," his friend had answered. "They'll be all right."

"If only Beth-ann could take them . . ." Daddy had sounded desperate.

"Why can't she?"

"She's got a summer job down the ocean, hostessing at the Bel-aire. She gets free room and board, so everything she makes will go toward getting us a house . . ."

Earl wheeled, turned left. He shook his head to clear the conversation from his mind. The other side of the tightrope was crowded. There stood the men in business suits who strolled along downtown passing Earl as if he didn't exist; the clerks who kept an eagle eye on him when he came in to buy a pack of gum; the

teachers who thought he was lazy or rude or stupid before they gave him a chance to speak; the black
teenagers who snickered at his cheap shoes and worn-
out jeans. Wayne was there too—Wayne, who didn't
care about anyone but himself, and who took care of
himself without anyone else's help. Remembering
him, Earl felt the pain return. He tried to think of
something else. "Frankie!" he shouted.

He turned onto the street, dodging trashcans, and
went right. Just as he crossed the boulevard he saw
Frankie ahead of him, sitting on the curb. He was
holding the sweatshirt in his lap.

"I couldn't keep up," he said.

"We took the bikes to Wayne's yard." Earl looked
around nervously, as if someone might be listening.

"Wayne hit the rabbit."

"That's because you wouldn't leave." Earl stood
looking down at Frankie, stroking the sweatshirt.
Earl's stomach clenched. "Wayne gave me six dollars."

"Wayne's mean."

Earl sighed. He pushed his hands deep in his pockets. "You're going to have to turn it loose, you know."

"Not it—her." Frankie's stubborn look was back.
"How come?"

"Because of Lula. She won't allow it." She almost won't allow *us*, Earl thought, but he didn't say that part.

Frankie refused to argue with Earl. "All right," he said. "I'll let her go."

"When?"

"In an hour."

"Here's a dollar," Earl said. "When you let her go you can get some candy."

"Okay." Frankie took the money without looking in Earl's face. "I'll let her go on my way home."

"See you." Earl turned. He looked back at his brother. Frankie might be dumb, but he'd hold on to something he wanted till hell froze over. "You're going to turn it loose, right, Frankie?"

Frankie nodded. "I'll let her go by the corner store."

Earl hesitated. He didn't want the rabbit to get killed. "How about in the park, near the bushes?"

"Yeah," Frankie said. He didn't look up.

Frankie wasn't going to let the rabbit go by the store or in the park, but he didn't say that to Earl. He didn't plan to let the rabbit go anywhere except at Lula's, in the bedroom. Earl could say what he wanted; Frankie wasn't going to give up the rabbit, no matter what.

He cut through the alley and approached Lula's house from the rear. The coal chute had a grating that could be pushed in, if you knew how, and he did that, sliding down to land next to the furnace. The bedroom he shared with Angela was in the front part of the basement. He went in and locked the door.

The room was large, with faded blue carpet over the cement floor. His bed stood under the window, but Angela slept on a mattress by the wall. Clothes, toys, and crayons were scattered everywhere. Frankie set the sweatshirt in the middle of the rug.

It took the rabbit a minute to get out. Then she darted under Frankie's bed. He got down on his hands and knees and looked at her. It was so dark under the bed he could hardly see.

"Come out," he said. "I want to play with you."

The rabbit was trembling.

"You don't have to hide, not now. Wait until Angela comes to hide."

The rabbit stayed still.

"Or if Earl comes, 'cause I told him I would turn you loose."

Frankie stayed in the room for the rest of the afternoon. He hung upside down over the bed and told the rabbit everything that was on his mind: how he wished Wayne and Earl wouldn't walk so far; how much he liked kindergarten; how he'd always wanted a pet. "But first I was too little, and then we couldn't afford it, 'cause Daddy was laid off. I wanted a cat, but Beth-ann's allergic to cat fur. She breaks out easy." Frankie smiled. He heard the front door open, and voices upstairs. "That's Lula and Angela . . ."

He thought of something important then. He went into the other room, closing the door behind him. Beside the furnace was a stack of bricks. He carried them two at a time into the bedroom and set them beside the bed. Then he built a wall around the rabbit eight bricks long and three bricks high. Afterwards he pulled the bedsheet down almost to the floor, so it was hidden. He checked his work from the far side of the room.

"They can't see you now," he whispered. "I have to go upstairs, but I'll come back to make sure you're all right." He moved a brick, and the rabbit's black nose appeared, sniffing. He stroked it once, put the brick back, and went up to the kitchen.

"Hey!" Some days Aunt Lula's wide blue eyes reminded him of Margie Tuck, who had sat by him in school, and could never remember what day it was, or what country they lived in. But Margie was blond, and neat. Aunt Lula's red-brown hair was messy. Tonight there were only flecks of lipstick left on her thin mouth.

"Just two more nines and I would have hit Lotto Express, Frankie. And I could have used it, let me tell you. Your dad's check is gone, and I forgot how much it costs to feed kids. Wayne used to eat at Taco Bell, but you all don't have money like Wayne did. He always had some way to make a dollar."

"What's for supper?"

"How about . . . spaghetti?" She said the word brightly, as if it were a new idea. Frankie didn't mention that they'd had spaghetti last night too.

"Earl's got a stomachache, and I can't find the Pepto-Bismol, even though I know I bought a great big bottle at the Super-Save last week." Lula stuck hairpins in her mouth while she fiddled with her hair. "I hope Wayne didn't come in here and take it," she mumbled. "Did he, Frankie?"

"No."

"He takes after his father." She sighed. "If there's one thing in my life I regret, it's marrying Bucky Bonner. Just talking about him makes me ill."

Lula opened a can of beer. "If I won a million dollars, I wouldn't give Bucky a single cent," she said.

She took the last pin out of her mouth. "Is my hair straight, honey? Hank Gates said he might take me to the races."

"Tonight?"

"Come to think of it, it was tomorrow night." Lula looked disappointed. She plopped down at the kitchen table. "I don't mind Hank Gates. If he asks me, I'm going. I thought you kids would fill the house with Wayne and Bucky gone, but something's missing."

"What?"

"I don't know—I guess I'm an old fool, still waiting for love. And maybe—just maybe—Hank's the one." Lula patted her bosom over her heart. She opened another can of beer. "I shouldn't be telling you this," she mumbled. "You're just a little kid."

"I'm seven."

"No, you're not. You just finished kindergarten."

"That's 'cause I stayed back, remember? I had to finish learning my letters."

"Wayne was seven once. He was so cute back then." Lula sighed. "He lost both his front teeth the same day."

Frankie's stomach growled. "Want me to help with supper?"

"No, thanks." Lula laughed. "I can make spaghetti in my sleep."

"Aunt Lula?" He turned his head away. Daddy used to say Frankie's face was like an open book. "Do you like animals?"

She got up and poured some water in a pot. "Once Wayne brought an animal home from school—a brown thing, like a mouse. He was supposed to keep it over the holidays. But Bucky got mad, and I called the teacher and told her to come get it. Wayne cried, I remember that . . ." She shrugged. "I didn't know it meant anything to him, Frankie. But he got over it."

She put the pot of water on the stove to boil. She found a can of spaghetti sauce in the cupboard and opened it. Then she belched. She put her hand over her mouth, too late. "I ought to tell Johnny to come get you kids," she muttered.

"He's on the Eastern Shore, remember? He's saving money so we can have our own house, like we used to."

"That would be nice, wouldn't it?" She wiped her hands on her skirt. "But I don't know about work, honey. I don't think the shipyard will call those boys back. If you ask me, the money days are gone."

Frankie felt his stubborns rising inside him. "We'll get a house somehow."

"What's life without dreaming, huh, Frankie?" Lula's words ran together. Her hug smelled of beer and perfume. "Go see about your brother now. I'll call you when supper's ready."

Earl was asleep on the couch, his knees drawn up to his chest. Angela sat beside him, watching *Sesame Street.* "That's my sister," she called when Maria came on. "See my sister, Frankie?"

"You don't have a sister, Angela."

"I do—I have a secret sister."

"I have a secret too." Frankie hadn't meant to say it. Angela stared at him. Her round face was grubby.

"You don't."

"I do."

"What is it?"

"I won't tell you."

"You have to." Angela stood up and stomped her foot. Thin brown curls fell across her face, and she shoved them back with one hand. "Tell me, Frankie. Pretty please."

"No."

"Pretty please with sugar and chocolate sauce."

He shook his head.

"Pretty please with sugar and chocolate sauce and Red Hots and M&M's."

"No."

"I won't say anything. I *swear*."

"You tell everything."

"I don't!" But Angela realized she had lost. She stuck her tongue out at Frankie. "I don't want to know your stupid secret anyway. I bet it's something bad. That's why Earl's sick. You all probably ate candy till your guts fell out."

Frankie shook his head, but he felt uneasy. Had they done something bad? Wayne and Earl hadn't talked that way, but it was true that Earl often got sick after their walks. On the other hand, Wayne said he took those bikes back. Not only that, but he gave Earl money so he could buy hotdogs and pop. One day he'd eaten more hotdogs than Frankie had ever seen anyone eat. No wonder he was sick.

The spaghetti was rich and warm. Frankie ate silently, but Angela talked between mouthfuls: "I got sick, too. Miss Cathy had to take me to the hospital."

Lula's eyes were closed. "That's nice."

Angela kicked Frankie's leg under the table. "Did you hear I went to the hospital?"

"Yeah." Frankie took another forkful of spaghetti. He wondered if Angela *had* gone to the hospital. Earl said Angela was the world's biggest liar, and usually she was, but now and then she told the truth. "What's wrong with you?"

"Cancer. They're gonna operate tomorrow, but I'll probably die. Then I'll go to heaven and be an angel."

"You could go to hell. That's where the devil lives."

"How do you know?"

"Mr. Tiptop told me. He knows all about the devil. He heard he came right through this neighborhood, wearing gold chains and driving a big car."

"How old was he?"

"Fifty-one."

Angela looked doubtful. "That's old. I didn't think he'd be that old, Frankie." She giggled. "Devil starts with a D."

"How do you know?"

"From *Sesame Street*. D is for David and Daniel and Donna and devil."

Frankie remembered Mrs. Chase showing him the letter D. He'd try to pay attention, but he kept waiting for her to put on the stereo. He traced a D on the tabletop. Did the curved part go this way or that way?

"Did the devil get drunk?" Angela grinned. "I saw that on *Sesame Street* too."

"You did not! Kid shows don't say that stuff."

"They do, too. One time Big Bird drank a whole case of beer. Then he burped and fell over."

"Angela!" Frankie *knew* that was a lie. But Angela smiled as if she didn't care.

Frankie put another forkful of spaghetti in his mouth. He swirled it from side to side, tasting the sweetness of tomato and cheese. He remembered the rabbit and felt happy.

Angela wanted Lula to tuck her in but Lula wouldn't wake up. Then Frankie said he would do it.

"There might be monsters." Angela was scared. "I think I heard one last night."

"I'll look all around—in the closet, too."

Frankie hurried downstairs and peeked under the bed. The rabbit was crouching behind the bricks, just where she was supposed to be. "No monsters!" he called.

Angela ran in and threw off her dirty clothes. She lay down on her mattress. "Look under the bed and in the closet one more time, okay?"

Frankie pretended to check. "All clear."

"Now tuck me in."

He pulled up the corner of the sheet. "There."

"Sing something, Frankie."

"I'll sing 'Just a Closer Walk,'" Frankie said. He started high, the way Mr. Tiptop had taught him, and let his throat open and his voice get fuller as he sang. He'd noticed that when he was feeling good the song took over as if it had a life of its own, and that happened now. He thought of the rabbit, safely hidden away. The song ended. Angela was already snoring.

He got down on his knees and peeked behind the bricks. "Tomorrow I'll give you a name," he told the rabbit. "Then you'll be completely mine."

THREE

Angela woke up first. She looked around the bedroom, hoping today was Easter or Christmas or Valentine's Day. But there were no cards or presents. Maybe the tooth fairy came, she thought, and she looked under her pillow. Nothing. Her dirty clothes were on the floor where she'd dropped them, and Frankie was on his back in bed, sound asleep. She sighed. There were fairies in the world, she knew, but they hadn't come this morning.

She realized she needed to pee. As soon as the thought hit her, she had to pee really bad. But she didn't want to get out of bed and climb the stairs to the bathroom. She waited to see if the feeling would pass, but it didn't, and a minute later a stream of warm liquid ran down her leg into the covers. She didn't mind the smell of pee, but grown-ups did. Lula had said she could make it to the bathroom if she got herself in gear, but Angela swore she wet the bed while she was sleeping.

The pee began to turn cold, so that the bed was uncomfortable. Angela got up, dressed herself, and went upstairs. Lula was sitting at the table with her eyes closed.

"Pink's my favorite color. Beth-ann loves pink too. She has a nighty that's pink, with little birds right here." Angela pointed to her chest.

"You'd think Beth-ann was queen bee instead of a cocktail waitress," Lula muttered.

"Earl says you hate her 'cause she's pretty."

"Don't say *hate*. I don't *hate* nobody." Lula shook her head, but she sounded grumpy. "Come on, Hank Gates," she said.

"Who's he?"

"He's a guy works in the pressing department. He wants to take me to the track."

"Can I go?"

"No way. You kids will be right here with someone looking after you."

"Earl can baby-sit us. He did once before, when Beth-ann was late from work. She called and ordered pizza, and we pretended we were in a restaurant."

"Maybe Earl." Lula nodded. "Or maybe Miss Queen Bee herself."

"She's working at the beach, remember?"

"She might come home weekends," Lula said. "I'll leave a message on her answering machine. She can call the laundry and let me know."

"Tell her to bring her curler set, so she can do my hair." Angela's voice rose to a squeak. "Tell her we'll watch TV and drink lemonade and play Old Maid."

"Old Maid . . ." Lula frowned. "You can tell her when she gets here." She poured Angela a bowl of Cheerios and sloshed some milk on top.

"Beth-ann buys Cap'n Crunch!" Angela said.

Lula sighed. "Come on, Hank Gates."

"Come on, Beth-ann!" Angela did a little dance on her way to the cereal bowl.

By the time Frankie got up, Lula and Angela had left. The rabbit was in the same place under the bed. Frankie moved a brick. "You can come out now," he said. "I heard the front door slam. Lula drops Angela at daycamp on her way to work, and Earl sleeps late."

The rabbit moved forward, sniffed Frankie's hand.

"If Wayne and Earl go looking for bikes, you and

I'll stay here," Frankie said. "I'll show you all the rooms in Lula's house. Wait for me while I get my breakfast."

The rabbit didn't move.

Frankie ate three bowls of cereal. Just as he was draining the last drop of milk from his bowl, he heard noises from the next room. He went in and saw Earl on the couch, mumbling and jerking his arms and legs. His eyes were closed. Suddenly he sat upright, and his eyes flew open. "The dogs! Get them back!"

"What dogs?"

"They were chasing me in the alley." Earl blinked. "I guess I was dreaming." He looked at Frankie and made his face go blank.

"You going out with Wayne?"

"No." For a second something uneasy flickered in his eyes. "If he comes, tell him I'm sick."

Earl pulled his knees up like his stomach hurt. Frankie stood still. He'd thought Earl would go so he could play with the rabbit. He couldn't take the chance of staying downstairs if Earl might come down.

"What are you waiting for?" Earl asked.

"Nothing."

"Then get lost." Earl rolled over on the couch, pulled his knees up, and closed his eyes.

Frankie went downstairs just for a minute.

"He wasn't always mean," he told the rabbit. "He used to roller-skate with me, and we'd race Big-Wheels on the sidewalk. Sometimes we made forts in the lot behind the used-car place. That was at our old house, before Wayne. Wayne is the one who hit you. He's dangerous, so never let him see you. Last year he killed a cat."

Later Wayne came to the door. Frankie knew who it was because he saw Wayne's big black shoes outside the basement window. He heard Wayne go *thump thump thump* on the outside steps and bang on the front door. He went up and peeked out the front room window. Wayne saw him.

"Unlock the door, Fat Frankie."

Frankie shook his head. "Earl's sick."

"Open the door!" Wayne yelled. He banged it hard.

Frankie didn't know what to do. He was afraid of Wayne, but he was afraid of Earl too, and Earl had said not to let Wayne in.

"It's my house!" Wayne yelled. "Open the damn door!"

"I can't!" Frankie yelled, and he ran away and hid till Wayne was gone.

"I didn't let him in," he told Earl later. Earl was watching TV and laughing.

"Look at that," he said, pointing to the cartoons. "Frankie, look!"

Frankie hung back. He had a question, but it was the kind that sometimes made Earl mad. "Did you change your mind about Wayne?"

"What?"

"Don't you like him anymore?"

Earl stared at the TV.

" 'Cause if you don't, we can do stuff like we used to. I know where Lula put our checkers." Frankie even thought of telling Earl about the rabbit, but he waited to hear what Earl would say.

"I don't want to play stupid checkers," he said. "I don't want to play with stupid you."

Later Earl did go out. As soon as he left, Frankie ran downstairs. The rabbit had moved to the other end of the pen. Frankie put out his hand, and the rabbit sniffed it. Frankie admired her smooth brown fur, and the black edgings on her ears and tail. He hung over the side of the bed, so she could see his upside-down face.

"Checkers is one game I like, and another one is marbles. Roy took every marble I had, but Daddy made him give them back. Then I played Beth-ann. I can beat Beth-ann.

"I wish Lula had a phone. If she did, I'd call Roy up and tell him to come over. He could take the bus, and we'd play checkers on the sidewalk." Frankie took a minute to scratch his head. Time moved slowly when he was alone in the house, but with the rabbit to keep him company, he didn't mind.

"Daddy said our new house will have a yard where I can have a pet. I used to want a kitten, or a puppy, but now I only want a rabbit, just like you."

The rabbit crept forward, rubbed its head on Frankie's hand. Its ears pointed forward, as if it were listening.

"I've thought of a name," Frankie said. "I'm going to call you Spot."

Later Frankie made himself a baloney sandwich and a glass of milk. He took the lunch downstairs and ate it on his bed. He told Spot about his favorite foods: hamburgers and pizza and chips and french fries and grape soda.

"Before Daddy left we had supper at McDonald's. I had two hamburgers and a chocolate shake. Daddy had a Big Mac, and Earl had two, and Angela had ice cream, and Beth-ann only had a salad 'cause she says she's fat. We walked to Lula's holding hands." Frankie paused.

"She was happy when we came. The first couple days we had fun—we went to Hardee's and the zoo. But Angela peed her pants, and Wayne saw Lula on the street and started cussing, and she cussed back. Then she gave us money to go to the movies while she played bingo. But the one we picked had monsters, so Angela cried, and Earl felt sick. The woman at the window wouldn't give our money back, so we went to the bingo hall early, and Lula said we blew ten dollars on nothing. The next day she bought beer— just this once, she said. She told us to play on the steps and stay out of trouble. That's where Wayne found us."

Frankie slid his hands close to the rabbit. She watched for a minute, then came forward and butted against them with her head. She seemed to want petting. When Frankie stroked her, she leaned forward into each stroke.

Earl didn't come home till late afternoon, and then, to his and Frankie's surprise, Miss Cathy brought Angela.

"She must have got some overtime," Miss Cathy said, when she heard Lula wasn't home. "I had to go somewhere, so I couldn't wait."

But Lula didn't come on the next bus, or the next, so that when the TV said nine o'clock Frankie and Earl and Angela were still sitting in the living room waiting. Then Angela remembered: "She said she might go out! And if she did, she'd get Beth-ann to baby-sit!"

"Why didn't you say so?" Earl's voice was shrill.

"Because I was thinking of something else—something real important."

"Beth-ann's gonna baby-sit us?" Frankie couldn't keep the grin off his face.

"I think so." Angela tried to remember. Earl gave her arm a shake.

"Beth-ann's working at the beach—that's why we haven't seen her. But where's Lula? Is she mad about something? Did Wayne talk to her last night?"

"You ask too many questions." Angela rubbed her arm.

"Crud!" Earl stood up. He stuck his fists deep in the pockets of his jeans and strode back and forth across the room. "I bet that sucker told her something."

"About the bicycles?"

"What bicycles?" Angela asked.

"Shut up, both of you!"

Frankie felt his stubborns rising. He thought of Spot, soft and quiet under the bed. She was turning out to be a better friend than Earl. He crossed his arms over his chest. "We won't shut up," he said. "We haven't even had supper."

Earl glared. He went into the kitchen and made hotdogs. When they were done he put them on a plate and slammed it on the table.

"I'm not your mother, Fat Frankie."

Frankie made a face behind Earl's back. He couldn't remember his mother, because she died when Angela was born. But Daddy said she was nice. Frankie bet she would have loved him more than skinny, stupid Earl. He felt tears come up, but he pushed them away.

The hotdogs weren't that good, because the squirt bottle let out too much mustard. When they tried to wipe it off, it soaked the rolls and made them wet. Angela said she hated hotdogs anyway. She drank a lot of milk to get the taste out of her mouth. Then she and Frankie found a can of Hershey's syrup and made chocolate milk. After they finished, Frankie asked, "If Beth-ann's coming, why isn't she here?"

"She went to Denver," Angela said. She had a brown milk mustache under her nose. "She's learning to dance the hula there."

"When will she be back?"

"February 59."

"That's soon, isn't it?"

"Yes," Angela said. "It's the day after tomorrow." She asked Frankie to tuck her in, like he did last night.

"I'll check for monsters first," Frankie said. He ran downstairs. The rabbit was safe under his bed.

Angela came in. She kicked the pile of dirty clothes beside her mattress. Her sandal touched something hard, and she dug in the pile and pulled out a broken yardstick. "Remember when I said I was thinking about something important?"

Frankie nodded.

"This is it."

"That's a broken ruler."

"No, it looks like a broken ruler, but it's really a magic wand." Angela lay down with the yardstick at her side. "You can tuck me in now."

Frankie pulled at the sheet. "That isn't *really* a magic wand, is it, Angela?"

"Yes, it is." She smiled. "Sing me a song, Fat Frankie. Sing the one you sang last night."

Frankie started "Just a Closer Walk," pitching his voice so he could reach the high and low spots. He opened his throat and let the song sing itself, like Mr. Tiptop said. But questions troubled him: Where had Lula gone? Could Angela do magic? How long could he keep Spot hidden under the bed?

"Beth-ann was supposed to baby-sit, but Earl and Angela say she's at the beach," Frankie whispered to Spot once Angela was asleep. He'd brought the rabbit water from the dry sink by the furnace. She sniffed it politely, then dipped her face to drink.

"Aunt Lula didn't come home. We don't know where she is." Frankie felt a knot in his throat. The rabbit nuzzled his hand. He moved a brick, and she climbed into his lap. "Do you want to hear me sing?" he asked. The rabbit blinked. Frankie thought that meant yes.

He wasn't sure what she'd like. Finally he chose the chorus from "Red River Valley" and sang it twice. Spot stared up at him when he was done. He rubbed his face against her back before he put her in the pen and went to bed.

FOUR

Addie wasn't really friends with Maynard, even though he lived next door, but she was glad he was with her when she found the empty rabbit hutch. The thing about Maynard was he never laughed at you. Instead he stared, with his little owl eyes, as if staring would help him figure things out.

Maynard was born in India, and came to Walnut Hill when he was two. Sometimes Addie thought his past had made him different. He didn't understand the rules of being a neighborhood kid: how to dress, how to talk, how to make friends; and he didn't know what was cool. He poked around, looking and listening and writing down what he saw and heard in a beat-up pocket notebook, as if life was a puzzle and once he found the answers, he'd fit in.

He was lonely, Addie knew. Kids at school teased him and called him nerd. She'd done it herself; until one day when she was lying in the hammock in the backyard, petting her rabbit. She'd heard strange noises coming from the hedge between their houses. She'd crept over and seen Maynard crouched inside the bushes, crying. After that she made a point of being nice to him, no matter what the others did.

It wasn't always easy. Maynard had weird ideas: he believed in wizards, dragons, coded messages from outer space. Once Addie asked him why. "Why not?" he'd answered, staring at her so hard she felt maybe she was the odd one. She'd blushed then, and gone back to playing with her Barbies; but she couldn't help thinking that life in Walnut Hill must be a little dull for him.

To make things worse, Dr. Glenn, who'd adopted Maynard, was also strange. He wasn't married, like normal grown-ups with children, or even divorced. He'd never had a wife, and he said he didn't care. He baked muffins on Sunday mornings, mended Maynard's clothes, and grew roses as a hobby. On holidays he dressed up in costumes he made himself: Santa Claus, the Easter Bunny, Cupid on Valentine's Day. Sometimes Maynard dressed up too. The sight of the two of them on Halloween—stocky Sherlock Holmes and short, scrawny Watson—made Addie's parents, the Johnsons, smile and roll their eyes.

Addie's life was as easy and comfortable as her own flesh. She could have walked blindfolded from the arched door in the stone wall to the swim club on Howard Street, to the deli and the pet store around the corner. The school was one block over, by the church; beyond it lay Davis Market, the video store, the library. Her best friends, Meg and Henry, lived near the western border of the hill. On summer days they hung out together, walking to the pool and stopping by the deli on their way home for french fries and Coke.

Then Meg went to the beach, and Henry left the same week for a month at camp. That Thursday morning when Addie came out to feed her rabbit, Maynard was sitting alone on his back steps. Addie cuddled Flag and kissed her ears. She saw Maynard glance at her, then turn away shyly. She wondered suddenly if he'd like to play. "Want to come to the pool?" she called.

"Me? You mean me?" He looked so surprised Addie almost laughed. "I *do* want to . . . I'll ask my dad, okay?" She nodded. His door slammed. A minute later he was back: "I can come! I'll be right over!"

"Actually, I haven't eaten." On summer days Addie had two blueberry waffles with butter and syrup for breakfast. "Why don't you meet me in a half hour?"

Thirty minutes later Maynard was there, carrying his towel, sweatshirt, and trunks. They patted Flag good-bye before they left. The pool was fun. On the way home, they dropped by the deli for a snack. When they got outside, Maynard stopped, took out his pocket notebook, and started to write. "What are you doing?" Addie asked.

"I'm collecting data." Maynard didn't look up. "Herb Renfrow ordered a tuna sub and chocolate milk; did you notice that? Yet in school he told Jenny he was vegetarian."

"Some vegetarians eat fish." Addie frowned. "*Why* are you collecting data?" she asked.

Maynard said, "I'm practicing."

"Practicing what?"

"What I'll do when I grow up. 'Cause I've decided what I want to be."

"What?"

"An FBI agent, like on *The X-Files*. If they don't

hire me, I'll be a private detective, with an office with my name right on the door."

"Oh." Addie blinked. She felt like she could see that door right there in front of her on Howard Street: *Maynard Glenn, Private Investigator.*

"What about you?" he asked.

"I don't know. To tell you the truth, I hardly ever think about it." Addie drank a swallow of Coke. She and Meg and Henry usually just talked about what they'd seen on TV last night; or who liked who in the fifth grade.

"Think about it now," Maynard said.

Addie stood there on the corner, closed her eyes, and tried to imagine being older. Where would she go off to work each day? She didn't want to sell insurance, like her dad. Her mom catered fancy parties; but Addie wasn't fond of gourmet food. "I like little kids," she said finally. "I could teach nursery school or kindergarten, I guess."

"You'd be good at that." Maynard stared at her. "Because you're nice. A lot of people aren't, you know?"

"Aren't what?"

"Nice," he repeated patiently. They came around the corner of her yard. Addie dropped her damp towel on the steps. "Let's go in the backyard," she said. "My mom's cooking, so she doesn't want us underfoot."

They sat on the swings and pushed forward and back, forward and back. Maynard watched Addie's blond braids as they jiggled on her shoulders. Everything about her seemed easy and contented, just the opposite of him. The toes of her white sneakers pointed as gracefully as a ballerina's when she leaned back in her swing. Maynard leaned back too. That's when he noticed the open door on the rabbit hutch.

"Flag?" Addie called. "I know I closed the cage," she murmured. She patted the straw inside, to see if the rabbit had burrowed under it, as she sometimes did on hot days. There was nothing. She yelled at Maynard, "Go get Mom—tell her to come quick!"

Addie tried to stay calm. She looked for Flag in the rose beds, and along the borders of the hedge. She checked the side yard. That was when she remembered the bicycles.

She'd gone riding with her dad last night. They'd pedaled the length of the neighborhood, then turned and circled back another way. When they got home, Mr. Johnson said to put the bikes away. Addie meant to do it, but *Full House* was on, and she never missed that show. She told herself she'd bring them in when it was over.

Mrs. Johnson hurried out the side door.

"I can't find Flag," Addie said. Her voice felt shaky. "I didn't put the bikes in the basement, and they're gone too."

The police came right away, but talking to them didn't make her feel any better. A pair of boys had stolen bikes last week in Orchard Crest, but nobody had any leads. They didn't think her family would ever see those bikes again. Even worse, they thought the thieves had taken Flag.

"When will I get her back?"

The men exchanged glances. There was something in the way they looked at each other—as if they were thinking things too bad to say out loud—that made Addie nervous. The tall one put his hand on her shoulder. "There's a chance, if you offer a reward . . ."

"We'll put an ad in tomorrow's paper," Mrs. Johnson said.

But Addie turned away. The phrase "There's a chance" bounced back and forth in her mind like a silent alarm. She'd hardly ever had a problem someone couldn't fix. Her best friend, Phoebe, had moved away after second grade, but Meg had come that same summer, and someone at church introduced them. Another time she'd left her jacket at McDonald's and someone stole it. That was upsetting, but she and her folks had gone to the store and bought another jacket just like the old one.

But you couldn't buy another Flag. Addie felt a twinge, as if something unexpected and upsetting had happened beneath the placid surface of a lake. Was it a bad dream? She pinched herself. When she took her hand away the soft flesh of her thigh bore an ugly pink splotch that didn't disappear for a long time.

After the police left, all Addie wanted was to go to her room, shut the door, and cry. But Maynard touched her arm before she went inside. "They're wrong," he said.

"Who's wrong?"

"The police." His eyes were peering into hers. "There had to be more than two."

"What are you talking about?"

He opened his notebook, checked his notes. "More than two thieves. Think about it: Flag isn't docile. Remember how she struggles if a stranger tries to pick her up?"

"That's true," Addie said slowly.

"Nobody could ride a bike and hold Flag, and there were two bikes. That means there was a third one who carried her."

"Oh." Addie nodded, but before he could say more she burst into tears, ran inside, and closed the door.

Maynard went home and lay down on his bed. Afternoon sun filtered through the blinds, lighting up books and magazines scattered across the floor. A bar of sunlight touched the Horoscopes column of the newspaper, which was folded on his pillow. Dr. Glenn laughed when he read these aloud, but Maynard suspected they might be true. He found his birth sign, Aries. The paper said: *Seek what is lost in a forbidden place.* Maynard sat up straight, heart thumping. Could this be a message about Flag?

FIVE

Friday Maynard spent the day at the hospital where his dad was working. The whole time he was thinking about Flag: Who took her? Where was the "forbidden place"? What could he and Addie do to get her back?

Saturday he got up early. He left a note on the kitchen table: *Gone for a ride—back soon.* He got his scooter out of the garage and headed for the door in the wall.

Hardly anyone in Walnut Hill was up. He stood alone at the entrance to the neighborhood and looked down on the city: skyscrapers and office buildings, warehouses and factories. Six blocks to the south was Grover Park. Maynard had asked to go there, but Dr. Glenn didn't enjoy exercise, and he said it wasn't safe for Maynard on his own. "Seek what is lost in a forbidden place," the horoscope said. Maynard headed down the hill.

He hadn't meant to stay in the park, only to cut through to the neighborhoods on the other side, but once he passed inside the gates onto the grass, kids swarmed around him like flies. A couple grabbed at the scooter, and someone else pulled on the sleeve of his new green T-shirt. "Look-it that boy's shirt! Look-it that scooter!" Maynard flailed his arms to clear enough space to breathe. All he could see were faces and hands. "Let me ride! No, *me!*" The kids scuffled around him. An older girl came to help. "Leave him be!" she bossed. She shook her fist, and they ran off.

"Thanks." He smiled nervously. "This is the first time I've been to Grover Park. I'm looking for a rabbit."

"A rabbit?" She shook her head doubtfully. "I hope it's not 'round here. After dark even the bugs hide, 'cause it's bad."

"Bad?"

She frowned at him. "Rough, boy. People get hurt, you know?"

"Oh." Maynard nodded. He took out his notebook and wrote that down. The girl moved away, staring at him as if he'd come from outer space.

He watched the other children play. There were games he recognized from school: hopscotch and dodge and jacks. A group playing tag swirled through the others like streamers in the wind. Several children were alone, as he often was himself. He watched them curiously.

To his left, a girl was playing with a broken yardstick. She pointed it first at one thing, then another. Her mouth moved in a silent rhythm, and she smiled as if she knew a secret. Her hair was uncombed, but there was something familiar about her. She clapped her hands three times, then spun around. Maynard blinked. She was wearing a sweatshirt with his school's name on it.

He rode toward her. He thought he might recognize her from recess, but she was younger than he was, and the preschool kids were usually gone by the time his class got out. Still, the school in Walnut Hill was small—he must have seen her once or twice. She eyed him warily.

"What the hell do you want?"

Maynard's jaw dropped. He didn't know any girls who cussed. "We go to the same school," he said weakly.

"We do not. I go to Miss Cathy's."

"But your sweatshirt says . . ." He stopped. Now

that he was closer it was clear that something wasn't right. The sweatshirt was too big, and the ruffled pink skirt beneath it was torn. The girl's pale, skinny legs were dirty, and her face wasn't washed, either. There were all sorts of kids at Maynard's school—white and black and Asian. But they were clean kids.

"What's your name?"

"None of your beeswax." The girl stuck out her tongue. Maynard started to back away, but suddenly she grabbed his arm and nodded toward the scooter. "Where'd you get that?"

"My dad gave it to me."

"Can I ride it?"

"No. Nobody rides this scooter but me."

"Don't be selfish."

"I'm not, only . . ."

"Only, what?"

"I don't even know you. I thought you went to St. James, but I changed my mind."

The girl eyed him thoughtfully. "Mr. Rogers says people can learn to share. He told me that's part of being friends."

"What do you mean, he told you?"

She smiled and seemed to relax. "He's my uncle."

"Mr. Rogers?"

She nodded. "I'm on his show sometimes. That's why I go to Miss Cathy's instead of regular school—so I can go to the TV studio."

Maynard peered at the girl. She didn't look like someone on TV. "Is he nice? Mr. Rogers, I mean?"

"Yes, unless he gets drunk. Then he'll knock your block off."

Maynard was shocked. "That's awful!"

She nodded solemnly. "My brother Earl's got a temper too. Once he punched me out. Then I broke his arm. He had to wear a cast for all of third grade."

Maynard knew about broken arms; he'd had one himself when he fell off the garage roof. But nobody wore a cast for the whole school year. "He didn't really," he said softly.

"He did." She nodded. "You can ask him."

"I think I'm leaving," Maynard said quickly. "See you later."

"Wait a minute."

"No, I have to go."

"Just wait." She reached quickly and grabbed the handlebars of the scooter. She looked right in his face. "I have a secret."

Maynard wanted to snatch off her hand and run, but he was also curious. She was hiding something behind her back.

"What?"

"This." She brought out the yardstick she'd been playing with before. "It's my magic wand—it puts spells on people." Her eyes shone. "I can put one on you."

His heart thumped in his chest. "No," he said, "you mustn't."

"If I don't, will you let me ride your scooter? Just once around?"

"If I walk beside you."

"Okay."

He got off, still holding the front bar with one hand, and she got on. Maynard caught a whiff of something that smelled like dirty underwear. She put her hands on the grips and started pushing. "Vrooooooom," she said, "I'm on a motorcycle!" She wrung her arms for speed.

That was when he saw the S-shaped ink stain on her sleeve.

He gulped and held on to the scooter for dear life. I made that stain, he told himself. I was watching

TV, and doodling with a Magic Marker. I knew I shouldn't, because the sweatshirt was new.

He closed his eyes, but when he opened them the stain was still there. He cleared his throat and found his voice somewhere at the back of it. It sounded dry and scratchy.

"That's my sweatshirt," he said.

SIX

Angela was surprised such a nice boy would be a liar. First he claimed she went to school with him. Later he said she was wearing his sweatshirt. She told him she found it wadded up near Frankie's bed. The boy kept staring at it, and at her magic wand too. After a while he took a notebook out of his pocket, sat down on the grass, and wrote something.

"Is it about me?" Angela couldn't read the words, because they were in cursive, but when he nodded, she swelled with pride.

The best part was, he invited her over. Other kids at daycamp went to each other's houses for parties or overnights, but Angela never did, because Lula didn't have time to mess with that. But Lula hadn't come home, and here was this boy, Maynard, saying, "Come with me."

"Where do you live?"

He pointed up the hill.

"Near McDonald's?"

"No, there's no McDonald's in our neighborhood." He looked sad. "My dad hardly ever takes me to Mc-Donald's. He doesn't like their food."

"He doesn't like McDonald's?" Angela couldn't believe she'd heard right.

Maynard shook his head. "He says it makes him fat."

"That's not true. Vegetables make you fat."

"Are you sure?"

"Yes. I saw it on *Sesame Street*. You should never eat too much broccoli, because you'll get fat, and you might throw up from the taste."

"It's awful. But eggplant's worse."

"Eggplant's terrible! It's against the law to give egg-plant to kids!"

"My dad wouldn't break the law," Maynard said doubtfully.

"He probably doesn't know about it. You see, egg-plant causes cancer, but just in kids. And if grown-ups feed it to them, special police can put them in jail."

"What special police?"

Angela paused, but only for a second. She gripped

the magic wand with both hands. "The Children's Police. They arrest mean grown-ups."

"My dad isn't mean! He didn't know better!"

"Then he won't get put in jail. He'll just get a spanking, so he won't forget and try again."

Maynard stared. He didn't think Angela was telling the truth. On the other hand, the idea of spanking grown-ups was intriguing. He imagined a pair of uniformed children whacking his father's broad bottom. He wondered if his dad would get mad or just burst out laughing. One thing was certain: if he found out Maynard went to Grover Park by himself, he *would* be mad.

"Don't tell my dad we were in the park," he warned Angela. "I'm not supposed to be here."

"The Children's Police say you can do whatever you want."

"Don't mention them, either."

"How come?"

"My dad gets upset if the police hit people."

"That's part of their job!"

"No, it's not. They're supposed to arrest criminals."

"Uh-uh. The police come afterwards and yell 'Get back in your house' and write reports."

Maynard gaped. After Flag was stolen, Addie had said, "All the police did was write reports." So Angela *did* tell the truth, at least sometimes.

They crossed the street at the boulevard. Angela hummed happily. She was invited to a friend's house! She glanced at Maynard out of the corner of her eye, hoping he wouldn't change his mind.

The walk seemed long. They passed the drugstore, but Maynard didn't have any money. "If only we could go to McDonald's," Angela said. Her rubber sandals were hurting the space between her toes, and her mouth was so dry she could hardly spit. "Are we almost there?"

"It's behind the wall."

"You ought to let me ride the scooter. I'm the guest."

"I already told you, nobody rides this scooter but me."

They passed through an arched doorway. Inside, the grass was so green it hurt Angela's eyes, and there was no trash. Maynard ran up the steps of a brick house and opened the door. He dragged his scooter through and signaled for her to follow.

Angela's feet stopped for a minute before they entered Maynard's house, even though her eyes went right behind him. It was as if her feet had a separate mind that thought: You don't belong here. Angela looked down angrily and told them: I do, too! She moved them slowly and deliberately over the doorstep and onto the carpet. She took a deep breath, hid her magic wand behind her back, and looked around.

The house was beautiful! In the front hall hung a lamp made of twinkling glass, and below it was thick, deep carpet, pale blue, like the dress of a princess. Music echoed from a room down the hall. Maynard started toward it. "You wait here, while I ask about McDonald's."

"No!" Angela was nervous about meeting Maynard's father—what was it she wasn't supposed to say?

"I thought you were starving."

"I am, but I want to look around."

"It's just a house."

"I know. And mine's a lot nicer, 'cause it's bigger, and it's pink. But I'd like to see your room."

"My room?" Maynard looked surprised. "Follow me."

The room was a disappointment, not because of the furniture (Maynard's bed had a blue and green comforter, with matching pillows around the top) but because the toys weren't as good as Angela thought they should be. There were no pink plastic ponies, no plush hug-me pets, not even a deluxe plastic home-maker's set with refrigerator and working oven. Instead Maynard had a box of blocks, some Legos, shelves of books and notebooks, and a machine sitting on a table. "That's my computer," he said proudly.

Angela frowned. "What does it do?"

"It keeps files and tells you things you want to know. It can play games, too. Come here, I'll show you how it works."

He pushed some buttons, and letters appeared on a screen. He made them come and go. Then he showed Angela how to write her name. He made pictures and let her choose what color she wanted them to be. He took out his pocket notebook, and copied things he'd written onto the computer screen. Then Angela's stomach growled. Maynard turned off the computer.

"I'll go ask about lunch."

"Hot damn." Angela got up too.

"Uh . . . why don't you stay here? I'll ask Dad to get enough for both of us."

"Why can't I come?"

"My dad doesn't like cussing." Maynard looked uncomfortable. "The best thing would be if you'd just keep quiet."

"All right." Angela fingered the wand. Let me go to McDonald's for lunch, she wished.

"Try to remember, Dad's never met anyone magic. He's used to normal kids. If you have to say something, make it boring and polite."

Angela nodded. She'd agree to anything that would get her a Happy Meal. But when she followed Maynard into the room where his father was sitting with a book, she was so surprised that she forgot what she promised. She thought Maynard's dad would look like him, but instead he was pale and fat, like Frankie. "My brother's fat too," she said.

Before Maynard could say anything, Dr. Glenn took off his glasses and turned around slowly. Then he smiled. "What's your brother's name?" he asked.

Angela realized she'd broken her promise. "Frankie Foster," she whispered.

"Miss Foster—I'm Dr. Glenn." He extended his hand, and Angela reached out to shake it. She saw suddenly that her fingernails were dirty, and there was a patch of something dried and grayish around her wrist. She hoped he wouldn't notice, and apparently he didn't, because he didn't say, "Go wash your hands." Instead he said, "Delighted."

"Could we go to McDonald's?" Maynard blurted. "That's Angela's favorite place."

"Angela Foster. Do you live nearby?"

Angela glanced at Maynard. He gave his head a little jerk, so she knew she was supposed to say yes. She nodded.

"And I see from your sweatshirt you go to school with Maynard."

Again Maynard jerked his head; so she nodded, even though she knew that was a *lie*.

"Carryout would be fine," Maynard said. "We'll stay in my room. That way we won't interrupt your reading."

"But I don't mind being interrupted," his father said. Angela noticed a bald spot on his head. She wondered if the hair had fallen out all at once or over a long time. She thought about asking, but he went on: "After all, this is Saturday. I was wondering where you'd gone."

"No place, really."

"I figured you were out sleuthing, maybe at Addie's."

"She didn't feel like talking."

"That's too bad." His father nodded absentmindedly. "But you found another friend."

Angela smiled.

"And it's fine. You haven't been to McDonald's for a long time. You needn't get carryout, either. We'll just swing past Angela's house and make sure it's okay with her mom and dad."

"That's all right. I can eat whatever I want."

"But I'd want to ask them, just to be sure."

There was a silence. Angela stared at Maynard, but she couldn't tell what she was supposed to say. His father wrote a note in the margin of his book. He closed it and set it on the desk.

"Shall we go?"

He stood up. Angela kept the wand behind her back. "You can't ask my mom and dad," she said finally.

"Why not?"

"My mom's in heaven, and my dad—" She started to tell about the Eastern Shore and getting money for a house, but then she remembered that she'd told Maynard her house was bigger than his. "My dad's visiting the President this week. He won't be home till Tuesday."

"Visiting the President?" Maynard's father asked

slowly. He frowned and looked at Angela again. Maynard said quickly, "I'll make us peanut butter and jelly. In fact, I think I'd rather have—"

"*Which* President?" Maynard's father asked.

"President Clinton. You see, he's my cousin, and sometimes he calls Dad and asks for help. Then we stay with my aunt Lula."

"Oh, my," the fat man said. He sat back down in his chair, put his glasses on, and adjusted them, as if Angela was not quite in focus. "Perhaps I could ask your aunt," he said finally.

"She didn't come home last night, so there's just Earl and Fat Frankie, and if you ask them, they'll want to come."

"Frankie. He's the brother you mentioned when you first came in."

"And Earl's my other brother. He's eleven. He's baby-sitting us while Lula's gone."

"You children are alone for the weekend?" Maynard's dad asked carefully. Something about his expression made Angela uneasy, and her voice wavered when she answered: "I'm having loads of fun. I went to Grover Park all by myself, and then I met Maynard, and he invited me over."

"You met Maynard in Grover Park?"

Angela nodded. She saw Maynard slip out the door without even waving good-bye. His father noticed he was gone. He looked at Angela again. Then he picked up the telephone.

Suddenly Angela knew no one was going to take her to McDonald's. She pulled the wand from behind her back and looked at it. The wand had almost granted her wish, but almost was worse than nothing. Tears blinded her. She heard Maynard's father say gently, "Don't cry. I'm going to call some people who will help you."

"You said you would take us!" Angela sobbed.

"I'm sorry. I didn't realize . . . maybe another day."

"I don't want to go another day!" Angela shrieked. She ran out of the room.

"Wait!" Maynard's father called. "Wait for me!"

She didn't wait. Carrying the wand, she ran as fast as she could out the front door and down the street.

SEVEN

Frankie sat on the stoop. He was so disappointed
he felt like crying. Beth-ann hadn't come after all,
and Lula's bed was still empty. Earl was curled up on
the couch, his eyes shut tight, and Angela was gone.
Frankie told Spot everything. Then he went outside.

It was already hot. He didn't mind the heat, even
when Lula fussed that the sidewalk was hot enough to
fry an egg. Fried eggs . . . his mouth watered. He
thought of Mr. Tiptop. He climbed down the steps
and hurried around the corner.

Mr. Tiptop lived in a basement apartment three
doors down from the store, next to what used to be
the Tiptop Shoe Repair. He was too blind to fix shoes
anymore, but he still had the cobbler's bench and all
his tools. These days he mostly sat and listened to music: jazz or classical, gospel or rock 'n' roll. When he
was young he'd been a backup singer on a couple of

Elvis songs, and he loved to talk about making those records, and what Elvis was like when he was young. "Before they ruined him," he said. "They killed that man years before he really died, Frankie—killed his soul. And they did it for one reason: the almighty dollar." Then he'd shake his gray head. Sometimes he'd pull out a bandanna handkerchief and blow his nose. Frankie didn't like to see him get upset. He'd tug on the old man's sleeve: "Play 'Rockin' Robin,' okay?" Then Mr. Tiptop would sit at the piano that was crammed into one corner of his crowded living room. When his fingers touched the keys, they seemed to come alive. This morning Frankie could hear Dixieland music drifting out the basement window. He banged on the door: "It's me. Frankie!"

Mr. Tiptop fumbled with the locks and let him in. His apartment was dark and smelled like boiled cabbage. Mr. Tiptop smelled funny, too: old and sort of moldy, Frankie thought. Once a month his sister came to clean the place. She spent the whole time fussing about the neighborhood: it was dirty and full of junkies. Why didn't Mr. Tiptop get a nice apartment in the suburbs, near her? He'd fuss right back. "I'd die of boredom in those big developments. Only

thing they do out there is shop and watch TV." His
sister rolled her eyes, but Mr. Tiptop hunkered down
at the table like an ornery old bulldog: "I'm staying
here!" When he heard that, Frankie was glad. Mr.
Tiptop was his best friend.

"I was just about to cook some ham and eggs," the
old man said. "Would you like some?"

"Yes, please." Frankie plopped down on the sofa.
He watched as Mr. Tiptop cracked six eggs into an
iron skillet and set two ham slices frying in a pan beside it. The egg yolks reminded Frankie of the yellow
balloons clowns carried in the city's Thanksgiving
Day Parade. Mrs. Chase had taught him a song about
Thanksgiving, and he sang it now: "Over the river
and through the woods . . ." Mr. Tiptop joined him on
the last verse. Then Frankie set places while Mr. Tiptop slid the fried eggs and ham onto a platter, and put
it on the table. Frankie sat down and clenched his
hands to keep from reaching for the food while Mr.
Tiptop said grace.

"Amen," he finished.

"Amen," Frankie echoed. He took three eggs, cutting them so that the thick yolks flooded his plate. He
pretended the pieces of the pink ham were boats on a
yellow pond. Smack, slurp, he ate the boats one after

the other. Then he thought of a song about boats and sang it: "Row, row, row your boat . . ." Mr. Tiptop sang the harmony, and they switched so that Frankie could try that, too. Then they sang it as a round. They sang until Mr. Tiptop was out of breath.

"Did you get enough to eat, Frankie?"

Frankie said, "Yes, thank you," even though he could have eaten a few more eggs.

"I have a new song for you this morning." Mr. Tiptop felt for the braille label on the spine of a record album. Elvis stared from the cover. "Never let them tell you the King couldn't sing gospel," Mr. Tiptop said. Frankie leaned back on the couch, listening to "This Little Light." He let his head rest on the shoulder of Mr. Tiptop's soft brown shirt. It reminded him of Spot.

"Did you ever have a pet?" he asked when the song was over.

"When I was a little boy, living outside of Memphis, we had a pair of hounds named Mabel and Jack. On hot days they'd lie underneath the house. It was my job to fetch them water and cornbread."

"Cornbread?"

"For them to eat. We didn't have the money for those sacks of dog food from the feedstore."

"Oh." Suddenly Frankie sat up straight. "What do rabbits eat?" he asked.

"Rabbits?" Mr. Tiptop looked puzzled. "Why, vegetables—greens and carrots . . ."

"I've got to go." Frankie stood up. "There's something I forgot to do."

"I'll see you later, Frankie."

He ran all the way home without stopping. The thought of Spot without food burned his cheeks like a slap. "Fat, stupid Frankie," he whispered angrily. He burst through the front door and ran down the steps to his room. He looked behind the bricks. Spot stared back.

"You're alive. Thank God!" Frankie rushed upstairs and rummaged in the refrigerator. In the bottom drawer he found a bag of wilted carrots. He took two and hurried toward the basement door.

"Where do you think you're going?" Earl put out a skinny arm from the back of the couch to block his way.

"Downstairs!" Frankie stuck the carrots under his T-shirt. Earl grabbed the lumpy spot and knocked the carrots down.

"What are you doing with those?"

"Uh . . . I'm hungry."

"They're all dried up."

Frankie just stood there. He couldn't think of what to say.

"Fat Frankie, you're so dumb you don't know garbage when you see it. If you're hungry, have some cereal." Earl shoved him toward the kitchen. Frankie went. He poured himself a bowl of Cheerios and forced them down. Then he stuck the carrots deep in his shorts pocket and headed for the basement.

"Where's Angela?" Earl had turned on the TV.

"I don't know. She was gone when I got up."

"Angela's gone?" Earl looked upset. "Gone where?"

"I don't know." Frankie shifted from foot to foot. He wanted to feed Spot.

"She's just a little kid," Earl said. He grabbed his sneakers and started putting them on.

"I'll check the basement—maybe she's hiding."

Earl nodded. "I'll look upstairs. Call me if you find her, okay?"

Frankie hurried downstairs and stuck the carrots behind the bricks. He watched for a second. Spot came forward, sniffed them, and started eating.

"Did you find her?" Earl's voice came from the top of the stairs.

"She's not in the bedroom. I'll check behind the furnace."

"Man, oh man," Earl said. "Check fast, Frankie."

Frankie went to the back of the basement. He looked for Angela under Uncle Bucky's workbench, by the dry sink, in the coal chute. He took his time. "Do the job slowly and carefully and you won't have to do it twice," Daddy used to say. He wondered where Angela *was*. Sometimes she claimed she was going on a trip, but Earl said she was lying.

"Did you find her?"

"No." He climbed the steps slowly. "Last week she said she was going to California. She said the ticket was in her pocket."

"Frankie!" Earl's face twitched. "That's one of Angela's stories. Now think—did she say anything last night about going somewhere?"

"She said she had a magic wand."

Earl sighed. He rolled his eyes at the ceiling, took a deep breath, and let it out slowly. "Anything else?"

Frankie tried to think. The funny thing was, as soon as he tried, all the ideas ran away like scared mice, so his mind was like an empty shoebox. He waited a minute, hoping an idea would edge back in, but it didn't. "I can't think of anything else. She was gone when I woke up. I came upstairs and the front door was wide open."

Earl looked scared. "We've got to find her."

"How come?"

"Don't you remember, in the letters?"

Frankie had to think for a minute. Earl read Daddy's letters out loud as soon as they arrived. They talked about life on the farm: driving the tractor, milking, sowing crops, even a flower garden Daddy had planted outside the window of his single room. But they ended the same way: "Look after each other until we're back together." Then he put a bunch of X's and O's for the kisses and hugs he was sending. Frankie nodded slowly.

"Let's go find her," Earl said. They hurried out the door.

EIGHT

There was no sign of Angela between Lula's and the park, nor on the cross streets, nor in the alleys behind the houses. No one in Grover Park remembered seeing a little girl with brown hair. When kids asked what she was wearing, Earl and Frankie had to say they didn't know.

"What next?" Earl muttered. His face was pulled as tight as a drawstring bag.

"I bet she's playing with someone," Frankie said. "She's probably at their house eating candy."

"You don't take candy from strangers. It might be poison, or they could be planning to kidnap you."

"If someone kidnaps Angela, they'll give her back," Frankie said.

"You don't know, Fat Frankie. You don't know how mean people can be."

"She's probably home right now," Frankie said.

· · ·

But she wasn't home. Earl was beside himself with worry. He tried to think who he could ask for help. The neighbors didn't get along with Lula, and Mr. Kim, who owned the corner store, was always busy with customers. Earl couldn't ask the police, in case someone had seen him riding a stolen bike and turned in a description. What good would it do to get Angela back if he ended up in jail himself?

Then he thought of Wayne.

Except for Friday, he'd helped Wayne with the bicycles every time he'd asked. Sometimes Wayne hit him on the shoulder and said, "Earl, good buddy, let's go out looking." When they got really good bikes, Wayne whistled under his breath and sometimes even told a joke. He always gave Earl five or six dollars. Earl knew those bikes were worth a lot more. Not only that, but Earl was putting himself on the line for Wayne. Wayne said, "These people have insurance. They'll get new bikes." Earl nodded and said, "Screw them." But inside he knew that taking those bikes was wrong.

Now Wayne can help me, Earl thought. And he's got wheels, so we can look farther away. To Frankie he said, "You stay here, in case she comes home."

"Look," Frankie said. He picked something up. "It's Angela's wand. It wasn't here before."

Earl snorted. "That's a broken ruler."

"She says it's magic," Frankie said. He stared at it to see if it would do anything, but it lay still in his hand.

After Earl left, Frankie went downstairs. He heard noises as he opened the door to his room. He stopped and listened. The noises stopped too.

He checked on Spot, who was sitting in her pen. Then he checked the closet and the bureau. He looked in the back room, by the furnace and the coal bin. He shook his head. "I might have imagined it," he murmured. "But Angela says I don't *have* any imagination."

"You don't," a muffled voice said.

Frankie almost jumped out of his skin. "Who's that?" he shouted.

No one answered.

Frankie trembled. He couldn't think of anyplace else to look, so he looked out the window over his bed. A pair of ladies' legs walked by, wearing white shoes. Legs don't talk, Frankie thought. He looked in the closet one more time. Then he pulled back the sheet on Angela's mattress. He knocked against the pile of dirty clothes beside the bed. The pile grunted.

Frankie stopped. "Clothes don't talk," he said.

Frankie wished Earl was home, but he wasn't. He wished anybody was home. He picked up a pair of dirty socks and moved them off the pile. Then he moved a shirt, a skirt, a damp towel. He set a dress to one side. Next he pulled a dirty sheet off the pile. He picked up a rubber sandal. There was a foot inside it! Frankie screamed.

"Shut up," someone said. The pile quivered and heaved. Angela's head came out one end. Her eyes were red, as if she'd been crying.

"You scared me to death!" Frankie yelled. "Where've you been? Earl's out looking for you now!"

Angela sniffed. It felt good to be the center of attention. "I went to Maynard's house."

Frankie figured she was lying. "Who's Maynard?"

"He's a boy who lives up the hill from the park. His house is real big." Angela opened her arms wide to show how big it was. "He has a be-puter in his room."

"What's that?"

"It's a box that can write and draw pictures."

Now Frankie knew Angela was lying.

"And his dad was going to take us to McDonald's, and I wished on the wand he would, but he changed his mind. That's why I came home." Angela's chest heaved. "The wand is broken," she said. Frankie could see she was about to cry.

"That wand only works for special wishes," he said quickly.

"What kind are special?"

"You have to figure that out."

"Oh." Angela cheered up then. She wriggled, thinking of the wishes she could try. "I'll make one for you, Frankie."

Frankie knew exactly what he wanted, but he didn't tell.

NINE

Wayne was asleep at Uncle Bucky's apartment. Uncle Bucky was asleep too. Earl pounded on the door for three or four minutes before Uncle Bucky slid open the locks and peered through the chain bolt. His eyes were rimmed with red.

"Who the hell is it?"

"It's Earl. Is Wayne here?"

"For God's sake, Earl. Come on in." Uncle Bucky's long hair and beard reminded Earl of a big, mangy dog. Bucky made a spitting sound to clear his throat. "Wayne's asleep in the bedroom."

The bed was piled so high with dirty clothes and blankets that Earl wasn't sure where Wayne began. He found a round part and shook it. "Wayne—wake up!"

Wayne wasn't glad to see him. He didn't even ask what Earl was doing there.

"Wayne—you got to help me. Angela's gone."

"Who?"

"Angela. My sister."

"Where'd she go?" Wayne wouldn't open his eyes.

"We don't know. Lula didn't come home last night. This morning the door was open and Angela was gone."

"She's probably at the track."

"Angela?"

"No, Lula. I don't want any part of her business. Her and me don't get along."

"I've got to find Angela," Earl repeated.

Wayne sighed. He let his head roll to one side. "She'll turn up."

"Can I take a bike to look for her?"

This time Wayne did open his eyes. "Hell, no. Don't you say nothing about those bikes in front of Lula, neither. She'd kill me."

"I got to find her, Wayne. Daddy said . . ." Earl felt tears come up behind his eyes.

"*Daddy said*," Wayne mimicked. "What are you, Earl, a baby?"

"Wayne . . ."

"Get out of here and let me sleep!" Wayne pulled the blankets back over his head and turned away.

There was no use asking Uncle Bucky for help. Even Daddy said Uncle Bucky would rather hit you than look at you. Earl slunk past his form, sprawled across the ratty couch, and went out the door.

He let himself run. The heat blew up into his face, and the smell of car exhaust was thick and choking. "It's going to be a hot one," people said. Earl didn't care. He could take the heat. It was the cold that got to him: cold air creeping up the sleeves of his winter jacket, creeping under the blankets at the foot of the bed to wrap itself around his legs until he had to pull his knees right up to his chest. He could shiver even in the heat, if he thought about certain things: mean dogs and ghosts and Freddy the killer from the horror movies. There was a coldness in those things, even in the idea of them, that chilled your insides. Earl turned right and kept running. Someone dodged out of his way, muttering, "Who's after you?"

He didn't know where he was going. Once he saw a girl Angela's size and he speeded up, but a mother came off the stoop, grabbed her, and pulled her away. His throat began to ache. What if your family had to suffer for what you did?

The first time he'd taken bikes was in June, after school let out. Wayne said, "Let's go somewhere."

They walked to the harbor. Behind the science museum was a park with fixed-up houses around it. There were two bikes leaning against a brick wall.

"They ain't even locked up." Wayne touched the silver one. "We could get good money for these."

Earl just stood there.

"If anything happens, you can say it was my idea." Wayne held his hands out, palms up. "If not, I'll give you a part of what I make."

Earl wanted to say no, but the bikes were beautiful. The tires were almost new.

"Come on, man."

He gave in then. His hands were shaking. He'd never stolen more than a candy bar; never ridden a fancy bike, either. For a second he thought it was broken, the way the pedals spun so smooth.

"Let's fly." Wayne took off. Earl followed, expecting any moment to hear someone holler from behind. They ducked into the alley, rode fast, swerved onto another street. Wayne crowed, and Earl rode up beside him and gave a high laugh that was a mixture of fear and joy. It had been easy, after all.

He wanted to keep the bike, but Wayne said no. He spray-painted it black, chained them both to the fence in Bucky's yard, and slanted a sheet of plywood over the top so no one could see. Earl felt sad, because the bike was spoiled. The next day Wayne gave him six dollars. He spent it on comic books and candy.

After that they went out a couple of times a week. Earl figured, I'm in it now. Sometimes it was fun. You'd be tingling with fear, then there'd come a moment when you knew you wouldn't get caught. Then he and Wayne would whoop like little kids . . .

He turned at the bottom of the hill. "Watch where you're going, fool!" Somebody shoved him to one side, and he tripped, landing hard beside a set of marble steps. The rowhouse behind them was brick, like the one next to it, but there was something familiar about the block. He got up, staring. Rollerblades, he thought suddenly. I was skating, and I wasn't supposed to come this far . . . He began to run, sprinting down one block, then another. The houses changed from brick to formstone and back again. Their wide basement windows held potted plants, stuffed animals, dolls from Poland and Russia. He remembered the old ladies yakking away in another language on the bench by the church. "Pretty, pretty," they would yammer when Beth-ann walked by. They grabbed at her silky skirts.

Daddy said she was working at the beach. But what

if she'd changed her mind, come home? Beth-ann would find Angela if she had to turn the whole city upside down.

"Right, then left," Earl said out loud. He dodged past a delivery van, past a couple of kids on Big-Wheels, up another set of marble steps. The door held a wreath covered with sweet-smelling bows. He banged on it, then rang the doorbell, but no one came. "Beth-ann!" he called. "It's me, Earl!"

No one came. He tried the door, but it was locked. Then he noticed a sign in the front room window: "For Rent."

"Beth-ann! Wake up!" He knocked so hard the door rattled on its hinges, but no one came.

TEN

Addie waited to hear from the police, but they never called. Friday she cried all day. But that night she got an E-mail message from Maynard, sent from the computer in his father's hospital office. It was labeled "Steps for Finding Flag." Addie read them over:

1. Make posters.
2. Interview neighbors and find out what they saw.
3. Search yard for clues.
4. Leave notices on the local newspage of the Internet.

She wiped her eyes. Having something to do made her feel better. As soon as she got up Saturday she went to the attic and carried down the cardboard box filled with family photographs. She sorted through them, found the ones she wanted, and spread them on her bed: close-ups of Flag standing on her hind legs to get a carrot; Flag sitting still; Flag peering over

Addie's shoulder into the lens of the camera. Addie couldn't help remembering the first time she'd seen her, one of four dwarf rabbits huddled against their mother in the pet-store window. She always looked in that window on her way home from the pool; she was used to seeing puppies or kittens lying asleep in the wood shavings, or frolicking with each other. Sometimes she'd go in and ask to pet one. The shop's owner, a shaggy, white-haired man named Mr. Bell, always said yes. But when she told her parents about the new arrival, they'd smile and shake their heads. "Puppies grow into dogs, and dogs have to be walked," Mr. Johnson said. "A cat's litter box has to be changed every day. Pets are a lot of work."

Addie would slump in her chair. She couldn't pretend she liked working. She was happiest lying in the hammock in the backyard, daydreaming; or sacked out on the playroom couch, watching TV.

But that was before Flag. That day Mr. Bell had picked up the baby rabbit and placed it in Addie's outstretched hands. The little creature sat up and turned gravely toward her. Its brown eyes weren't afraid, just curious. "That one's lively," Mr. Bell said. "She's the leader of the gang."

Addie ran one finger down the rabbit's soft back. "Are they hard to take care of?"

He shrugged. "You have to feed and water them, and clean the cage out now and then. Course they like contact—they'll get real attached if you treat 'em right."

"How much do they cost?"

"Fifteen dollars, but she's not for sale. Too young to leave her mother for three more weeks."

"I'd have to buy a cage . . ."

He shook his head. "Most people build a hutch. All it takes is some scrap wood and rabbit wire, a couple of hinges for the door, a good latch. You could do most of it yourself."

"Not me," Addie said right away, but when he reached out to take the baby rabbit she wanted to pull her hands up tight against her chest and hold it there. "Can I come back and pat her again?"

"Anytime." He adjusted his wire-rimmed glasses, squinted down at her. "That one seems to have taken a shine to you."

Addie walked home without stopping at the deli. She looked in the basement: there were some pieces of plywood left from one of her father's projects, and a mason jar held hinges of different sizes and shapes. Nails were in a coffee can, but there was no wire. She called Henry to ask if he had any. He looked in his backyard and found some trellis from his mom's garden. "But I'd better ask her," he said. "What's it for, anyway?"

"I'm making something."

Henry seemed surprised. But Addie didn't tell him about the baby rabbit, not then. If she told, the dream might disappear, like a cloud floating past and out of sight.

She spent that afternoon and part of the next day in the basement, hammering away. The hinges went on crooked, and the corners of the box jutted out at odd angles, like something from a cartoon. Addie ended up buying wire from the hardware store, but the staple gun jammed, and a nail she drove in to hold the wire split the side of the hutch into two pieces. She felt like giving up so many times. And when she finished, the rickety, misshapen box in front of her didn't look fit to hold a stone.

"What's this?" Mr. Johnson asked when they were putting the bikes away that night.

"Something I was working on . . ." Addie had turned red. She'd hoped to show her parents something beautiful and strong, so they'd know how serious she was about the rabbit, how much she wanted her. Her dad poked the cage with his running shoe. A piece of wood fell off and clattered to the cement floor. Addie put her hands to her face, but tears edged out anyway. Mr. Johnson looked astounded.

"What's wrong?"

"You broke my rabbit hutch."

"Is *that* what it is?" He seemed sorry, and puzzled. She nodded miserably.

"But we don't *have* a rabbit." He faced Addie. "Do we?"

"Not yet."

"This sounds like something I need to hear about," he said gently. "Why don't we go upstairs, and you can tell me the whole thing?" She nodded, still crying, but inside she was shouting, *He didn't say no!*

They worked it out this way: she had to earn the fifteen dollars herself. Only then would Mr. Johnson help her build the hutch. At first Addie didn't know where to start. She'd never wanted anything enough to work for it, and her household chores—making her bed and setting the table—didn't count as paid jobs. Weeding the flower beds, she pulled up three daylilies by mistake and ended up with a measly two dollars. It's not worth it, she thought, and she tried to put the rabbit out of her mind. Once, passing the pet store, she walked on the other side of the street. But something pulled her back, like a magnet, and she ended up standing outside the window until Mr. Bell opened the door.

"Could I . . . could I see her?"

"They're in the back. Vet's coming to give them a checkup."

"Oh." She tried to pretend she didn't care.

"Two more weeks and they'll be ready to go."

"Two weeks . . ." She smushed the toe of her sneaker against the tile floor. "Could I take a peek? In the back, I mean?"

"I know what you mean." He sighed. "Go ahead."

The feeling was still there. Addie's rabbit crouched in the center of the cage, head high. Her eyes followed the movement of her brothers, but when they came too close she leapt straight up over their heads and whirled around, landing lightly on all four paws. Her tail shot up behind her like a brown flag. Then the rabbit noticed Addie. She hopped to the side and stood, her front paws balanced on the wood barrier.

"It's me again," Addie stammered. "I'm saving

94 ·

money, so I can . . . get you." She thought saying "buy" made the rabbit sound like a toy, or a bag of groceries. "My dad and I are going to build a hutch, as soon as I've saved the money. I already have two dollars."

She reached out quickly and stroked the little animal. To her surprise, the rabbit leaned forward, as if she liked that.

"I'll be back," Addie said quickly. Walking away, leaving Flag—that's what I'll call her, Addie thought, Flag—was like leaving a part of herself behind.

Lawns, dishes, baby-sitting, hauling trash: the next weeks were long and hard. At night Addie sank into her beanbag chair too tired to pick up the remote and turn on the TV. On a Thursday, she collected her final pay. That night she and her dad rode to the hardware store for supplies. It took two days of cutting and measuring, hammering and stapling, before the hutch was done. Addie spread the bottom with straw and set out bowls of food and water.

The odd thing was, Flag seemed to understand about Addie ahead of time. When Mr. Bell picked her up that day, she bit him gently on the thumb; and she scratched Meg with her front paws. She was indifferent to Mrs. Johnson, unless she brought carrots, and when Addie's dad approached, Flag turned her back and looked in the other direction, as if there were something more interesting over there. It was only for Addie that she turned and scampered to the cage door, only Addie's stomach she rested on so peacefully as they lay together in the hammock, only Addie's voice that made her kick up her heels and leap for joy. It was as if there were special people who loved rabbits, and with whom rabbits felt at home: *rabbit people*. They had no distinguishing characteristics, but rabbits could tell them apart from everyone else.

The telephone rang. Addie started, then stared at the pictures on her bed. I've been daydreaming, she thought in disgust; I haven't got a single poster done.

"Addie! It's for you."

She picked up the phone in her dad's study. Maynard sounded rushed. "I can't talk now, 'cause I'm grounded for the day, and I'm not supposed to use the phone. But I need to see you first thing tomorrow."

"How come?"

"Something happened . . ." Addie heard a sound in the background, then, in a low voice, Maynard said, "I've got to go."

"I'll be here all morning."

The phone clicked off.

．　　　．　　　．

He came at eight o'clock. His eyes had that intense look that sometimes scared Addie, and the first thing he said was, "We need to talk. Someplace private, where we won't be overheard."

Addie opened the door of the hall closet and switched on the light. They pushed back behind the winter coats, and sat against the wall. Maynard took out his pocket notebook. He riffled through the pages.

"I went to Grover Park looking for clues about Flag. While I was there, I met a girl. Her name is Angela."

"You went to Grover Park all by yourself?"

He nodded. "That's why I got grounded." He explained about the horoscope, staring at his hands instead of Addie. "I know most people don't believe that stuff, but I thought it was worth a try . . . Anyway, this girl knows all about the police. She says all they do is write reports."

Addie felt a sinking feeling. No wonder the police hadn't called.

"Right now she's living with her brothers and no grown-ups—at least until her dad comes back."

"No grown-ups!"

"There's more!" Maynard leaned forward. "She says she's magic."

Addie frowned. He shifted uneasily, as if he guessed she was skeptical.

"I didn't believe her at first. She's got this broken ruler she plays with, and she calls it her magic wand."

"I used to play that game when I was little," Addie said.

"I know—but there was something else. She had my sweatshirt."

"Your sweatshirt?"

"Yeah, the one that says 'St. James School' on the front. I know it's mine 'cause there's this funny ink stain on the sleeve."

"How'd she get it?"

"I don't know. That's why I thought . . ."

But Addie shook her head. "There's got to be some other explanation." She sat for a minute, pondering. "When was the last time you had it—the sweatshirt, I mean?"

"I took it to the pool, though I don't actually re-member having it once we got out of the water. I might have left it in the changing room."

"And somebody could have found it, and given it to her." Addie nodded.

"She said it was her brother's."

"So maybe he found it there."

Maynard hesitated. "I doubt it. You see, Angela's different from the kids in the swim club, and I bet her brothers are, too."

"How?"

"She . . . she doesn't look like girls in Walnut Hill. Partly it's her clothes—they're messy and dirty. She smells like she doesn't take a bath every night." Maynard wrinkled his nose, remembering. "She doesn't act like girls here, either. She cusses and she goes wherever she wants to and she makes up stories. And she knows about different stuff, like the police."

"I wonder how she knows about that . . ." Addie mumbled. But she wasn't thinking too hard about it, not now; because in the back of her mind a memory had taken root and was wedging its way up through the tangle of questions and worries. It was a memory of grass, seen from the corner of her eye as she was heading somewhere else. She put her hands over her face, thought back. There was a softball there, and some comics, and on the far edge of the picture, the rabbit hutch. So it was her own yard she was remembering.

"Addie?"

"Just a minute . . ."

She let the image drift forward. It *was* her yard, and there were bikes in the foreground, and the swing set, and the hutch, and little things: the ball, and the comics, and to the left, beside the hutch, a streak of color. I should tell him to pick that up, she chided herself. He's supposed to take it with him, to put on afterwards . . . Addie's eyes flew open. "You dropped it in the yard!" she blurted.

"What?"

"The sweatshirt! It was lying in the yard, beside the rabbit hutch."

Maynard stared.

"Somebody took it when they stole Flag! They got it from my yard!"

"Not Angela," Maynard said quickly, but in the dim light he looked shaken. "She'd never been to Walnut Hill, I could tell. She said she'd never seen so much grass in her whole life."

"Maybe not Angela, but someone she knows. They got that sweatshirt from the yard! They took it while they were stealing Flag!"

ELEVEN

They didn't tell their parents what they'd figured out. Addie felt her folks would simply call the police. "But Dad says they're so busy with holdups and murders that there isn't much time for anything else." She turned toward Maynard. He'd never seen her blue eyes so determined. "That means we'll have to catch the thieves ourselves."

Maynard nodded. He suddenly felt nervous, almost giddy. Here was a chance to prove himself, and help Addie too. But there was another reason for keeping quiet. He wanted to find Angela.

She was, he thought later, the most unusual person he'd ever met. She wasn't worried about how she looked, or what she said, or whether she'd fit in; she just went ahead and did things, whether other people liked them or not.

He talked to his dad about Angela. Dr. Glenn was in the backyard Sunday afternoon, shoveling compost around his roses. His thick white legs stuck out from under a pair of plaid Bermuda shorts. Maynard sat on the ground, gazing at the forest of little hairs above his dad's socks. "You should have taken her to McDonald's," he said.

"We've been through that," Dr. Glenn said patiently. "I can't take your friends out without their parents' permission."

"Her dad would have given it, once he got back."

"You don't know what he would have done. I can't imagine a man who'd leave three children alone all weekend. I called Social Services and told them everything the little girl said."

"She was having fun," Maynard argued. "I'm older than her, a boy, too, and I hardly get to do anything."

His dad shot him a warning look. Maynard stared straight ahead. He put his arms around his knees and rested his chin on top of them. Through the hedge beyond the flower garden he could see bits of Addie's yard, like pieces of a puzzle. How did Angela fit in?

He had to find her fast. He'd already taken the phone book to his room and looked up Foster. There was no listing for Angela, Lula, Earl, or Frankie. He typed "Grover Park" into the computer's geography program. It printed out a map of all the nearby neighborhoods. Maynard put it in his pocket. Tomorrow I'll look for her, he thought; not in the park, 'cause I promised Dad I wouldn't go back there, but near it. He didn't say anything about that.

As soon as Dr. Glenn left for work the next morning, Maynard told the housekeeper he had to do an errand. Then he grabbed his scooter and took off. He rode to Grover Park and pulled the map out of his pocket. He found the intersection where he was standing. "I usually go that way," Angela had said, pointing; so Maynard did, too.

He rode past two blocks of brick rowhouses, then reversed direction on the next block down. Nobody in the neighborhood seemed to have heard of Angela, Frankie, Earl, or their aunt Lula. Some people wouldn't speak to Maynard at all. "Beat it!" said a teenager with a scar on his forehead, and a dark-skinned man with watery eyes stared right past him as if he couldn't hear or see. Maynard noticed that the houses were changing: in this block there were two with boarded-up windows, and a third was listing to one side as if a strong wind might blow it over. He took out his notebook and wrote down what he saw.

The people seemed different, too. More and more of them were outside, instead of in—sitting on steps, leaning against a parked car or the wall of a corner store. Maynard wondered vaguely why they hadn't gone to work, like his dad and Mr. Johnson. They must not be planning to go, either, 'cause they weren't wearing suits and neckties. Maynard thought suddenly: these are poor people. Someone—not his father, but old Mrs. Owen, who lived up the street, had told him that India was a country of poor people. Maynard shivered. If he'd stayed there, maybe he'd be sitting on his step in tattered clothes, like a woman he'd just passed. His heart beat faster, and he pulled the map out of his pocket. The printout, with its neat diagrams, seemed like a friend. A police car came around the corner. The officer stopped and rolled down his window. "Do you know where you are?" he asked.

"Yes," Maynard said, "I have a map." He kept going. The policeman watched him for a minute, then rolled up the window and drove away.

Maynard went on. He must be looking in the wrong place. Angela had said her house was bigger than his; but he hadn't seen a detached house since he left Walnut Hill. A dog rushed at him, baring its teeth; he sucked in his breath and shouted, "Go away!" The dog turned and ran.

He asked more people: "Do you know a family named Lula, Angela, Earl, and Frankie Foster?" "Never heard of 'em," some answered, or just, "Uh-uh." A kid his age said, "I'll show you if you give me money."

"How much?" Maynard had some change in his pocket.

"A hundred dollars." The boy sneered and ran away.

Maynard took out his map and checked off another block. He was tired and thirsty, but he couldn't help thinking, I'm on my own! He looked carefully at the metal numbers on the doors of the houses, noting how they rose in sets of two: 2122, 2124, 2126.

"Hey, you!" The boy was back with a group of friends. "We found those people."

"You did?" Maynard stared at them. They weren't smiling, and one had a glint in his eye. Maynard knew bullies from the playground at school. He turned, but not fast enough. One of them grabbed the handlebars of the scooter.

"Give it up," he said in a low voice.

Maynard's heart began to pound. He took a deep breath: "No way."

"Give it up, I said!" Another boy grasped him from behind, while the one in front slammed his knuckles with a stick. Maynard yelled. The third boy pounded his shoulder. "Give it up, geek!" Maynard clung to the scooter with his legs and started hitting back. He landed a solid punch on one boy's nose. "Break it up!" someone shouted. "Off you!" one of them answered, but a moment later they kicked Maynard hard and sprinted away. He held tight to the scooter. "You okay?" somebody asked.

"I . . . I . . ." Maynard focused on the ground. "I'm looking for someone."

"Who?"

"Angela." His voice came out squeaky, 'cause he felt like crying. "Her brothers are Earl and Frankie, and their last name is Foster."

"Foster . . ." Maynard looked up and saw a middle-aged man with a stubbly chin. "I don't know them."

"Their aunt's called Lula."

"Rose, you know somebody name of Lula?"

"Naaaah," someone answered from inside the window of the nearest house. "Ask Harry."

"Harry lives down the corner . . . you can bang on the door."

Maynard blinked back tears. The man must have noticed. "Come on, I'll take you," he said.

Harry was old and feeble, and his voice was as high as Addie's. "Only Lula I know used to live around the corner from the store. But I heard she's gone, least that's what they said at the bar. Moved in with a boy from work."

"Did she have kids?"

"Just one—a big boy, mean as a snake. I wouldn't go 'round him if I was you."

Maynard sighed. She didn't sound like the Lula he was looking for. "Where did you say she used to live?"

"Down there, boy." The old man peered at him as if he was an idiot, then pointed. "Right down there."

"Around the corner from the store," he'd said. Maynard found the store easily; there were a bunch of kids sitting on the stoop. He checked the street signs: Lakeland and Hoyer. The rowhouses were small and shabby. Two were boarded up, and the one next door had a scraggly flower bed out front. The kids were muttering in low voices. I should ask them, Maynard thought; but they didn't look friendly.

Just then a teenager loped across the street. He was tall and thin, with a long nose. At the neck of his yellow tank top was a scattering of dark hairs.

"Ready to go?" He spoke to a redheaded boy who was sitting with the others.

"You got to give me my share this time. I need the money."

"Stop whining, would you? You always get your share."

"This time I need it," the boy repeated doggedly.

The teenager shrugged. His voice was cold. "We'll discuss it, okay? Are you coming or not?"

They walked right by Maynard. He saw their eyes as they came close: hard, blank eyes. He watched as they disappeared down the street. Then, clutching his map, he turned his scooter around and raced for home.

TWELVE

There were two reasons Earl was going with Wayne. One was money. He'd already spent the fourteen dollars in Lula's bureau at the corner store, bringing home Cheerios, milk, hotdogs, spaghetti, and spaghetti sauce. There hadn't even been enough for hotdog rolls. Angela wouldn't eat her hotdog plain, so Frankie ate it, and then she cried because there was nothing else for supper.

That was the other reason: the little kids. They were driving Earl crazy. They thought that because he was oldest, he'd be able to make things right. He couldn't admit that he didn't know how. He felt like he and Frankie and Angela were invisible, lost among the rushing business of the world. Wayne was, at least, a connection.

"So you found the kid?"

Earl nodded, his teeth clenched.

"Told ya." Wayne kicked an empty bottle into the middle of the street. "Watch somebody cuss when they pop it," he told Earl. Then he asked, "Lula still not back?"

"Uh-uh."

"Maybe I'll move in. We can party." Wayne cuffed Earl on the shoulder like they were friends. "Bucky's no dream to live with, let me tell you. He like to tore me up for playing my own stereo." Wayne showed off bruises on his arm and neck. "I was hollering like a stuck pig."

Earl thought fast. The last thing he wanted was Wayne there, too. "She's coming back," he lied.

"I'll believe it when I see it. When Ma's drinking she just drifts away. I been through it, and I know."

"Why'd she want us, then?" Earl muttered angrily.

"I guess she was lonely. Then she slipped. She can't help it, really."

"If only Beth-ann were here . . ." Earl said it low because he didn't want Wayne to hear. Earl knew Beth-ann could save more working at the beach. But saving money wasn't that easy: just last week Daddy's old Buick had thrown a rod. Now the engine had to be rebuilt. *Bad luck,* he'd written Earl. *We'll fix it and move on.* But to Earl bad luck seemed like a cancer;

once it got a grip on you, it just kept turning up. He shivered.

"You sick or something?" Wayne was staring at him. "I don't want to catch nothing."

"I'm not sick," Earl said. "I'm fine."

They walked to Hopkins Square. "Yuppies," Wayne explained, pointing out the flowering plants and brightly painted front doors. "They got money." But the backyards had stockade fences around them, and the gates were locked. Wayne pulled himself up by his hands to look over the top of each fence, but Earl knew no matter what he saw they'd never get a bike over a seven-foot fence. Wayne cursed. "They even got locks on their stupid barbecues," he said. He spat on the ground. "We ought to take something just to show them."

"Sounds like there's nothing to take," Earl said. He felt relieved.

"I'm not done yet," Wayne said.

But there wasn't anything—even most of the cars were gone, and the ones that weren't were locked up tight. Wayne said for ten bucks you could get a tool that pulled the rubber lining right out of a car window. Then you hooked a wire through and opened the lock. But Earl didn't see anything valuable in those cars anyway—just a pair of sunglasses, a map, a baseball cap. Wherever these people came from, someone must have warned them about crime.

They went to Greektown. The bars were open, and sailors were singing and dancing, their arms around each other's shoulders. "They got money, but look at us, we're Americans, and we got nothing," Wayne said. Earl watched the sailors from behind the door. They looked like they were having fun. One saw him and beckoned for him to come in, but Earl quickly backed away. He felt nervous around people who spoke a different language. What if they were talking about him?

"This way," Wayne said. There were some bikes around the restaurants and the art gallery, but they had good locks, and they had stuck them through the front wheel, too, so you couldn't slip it off and run. They went through the alley onto the wharf. Two freighters were tied up, but they had watchmen on the foredecks. Wayne cursed. "I hate this town," he said.

Earl was getting tired. "Maybe we should go back."

"Not yet. You ain't the only one that's broke." Wayne spun around. "Follow me."

This time he led Earl toward Downtown. They cut through Front Street, where the chemical plant used to be. The lot was fenced off, with big warning signs: "Danger! Toxic Substances!" They passed the diner near Earl's old house. "Where we headed?" Earl asked.

"To the parking lot under the expressway. A bunch of bums sleep there with their bags of stuff. Some of them get Social Security. If you wait till they're alone or drunk, you can take it without them batting an eye." Wayne stared at him. "You ain't chickenshit, are you?"

"No, but I got to go back. I left Frankie and Angela."

"They'll be all right. I need cash. There's nothing to eat at Bucky's."

"I don't want to," Earl said.

"You just come and watch out. You don't have to touch nothing."

Earl hung back. That's what Wayne had said before, but it always turned out different.

"Will I still get money?"

"If I get twenty bucks, I'll give you ten." Wayne's voice had gotten ugly. He looked like he might slap Earl any second now.

Earl followed Wayne.

They came to the underpass. Like Wayne had said, there was a parking lot, and on the far side of it were a couple of mattresses and a plastic lounge chair. Some of the mattresses had blankets on top, and one had an open trash bag on it. Earl could see it held clothes. Across the way were more bundles of rags and blankets, and an old trash barrel that stunk like wet cinders. "They keep a fire in there, on cool nights," Wayne said.

"Where are they?"

"At the soup kitchen by the library. Same place you and me are going to end up, if we don't get lucky."

"Can kids go there?"

Wayne nodded. "Ma took me a couple times, when she'd drunk up all the money. It's embarrassing, you know, man?"

"Yeah."

"You got to choose: that or this." Wayne shrugged. "It's survival." He stopped suddenly and pointed. "There's one, Earl."

A man was slumped against the concrete wall of the underpass. His head was nodding so that Earl couldn't see his face, but his body looked frail. In one hand he clutched a zippered cloth case.

"The money's in there," Wayne whispered.

Earl didn't say anything. His heart was racing.

"Come on," Wayne said.

"I told you, I'm not hurting nobody. I'm only going to keep watch."

"Come on!" Wayne's voice was sharp. Earl followed him, looking back and forth to see if someone was coming.

Earl willed the man to wake up, but he didn't. He smelled like pee. As they got close Earl could see tiny broken veins in his face and neck.

Wayne snatched the case. "Got it!" The man groaned, then opened his eyes and yelled. The boys took off.

Earl ran after Wayne, who'd stuffed the case inside his shirt. They ran for a few blocks, then Wayne stopped and squatted behind a brick wall. Earl saw that his hands were shaking. The zipper stuck on the case, and Wayne ripped the seam and dumped the contents on the ground. There was a razor, some soap, a couple of cigarettes, matches, a dollar bill, and some change. Wayne picked up the money. "Only a dollar thirty," he said in disgust. "Man, oh man . . . he must have had his wallet in his pants."

"I'm not going back," Earl said. He felt like he might throw up.

"A lousy dollar—and a razor. As if that jerk needed to shave." Wayne's hands were still shaking.

"Maybe he doesn't have a wallet."

"They get Social Security."

"Maybe it's spent."

"Yeah. Probably blew it on dope." Wayne stood up. He hurled the case into the street. "Screw him. Next time we pat them down to see where they keep the cash."

There isn't going to be a next time, Earl thought, but when he looked at the few coins in his hand, he wasn't so sure.

They split up on the way home. Earl bought himself a Coke with the change, then stomped the can and left it on the sidewalk. His stomach hurt. He trotted, then ran along the avenue, passing the street where they used to live. If he stopped and stood on his tiptoes, he could see their old house. He could remember every piece of furniture, every picture in the living room, the flowered cups in the built-in china closet, the cast-iron sink in the kitchen where he'd sailed his toy boats and Mama sang to him while she changed Frankie's diaper. What would she think if she could see him now?

A few blocks later he turned right. A high-rise tow-
ered on one side of him, and he realized he was bor-
dering the harbor, near Downtown. The high-rises
were new; most of them had balconies and swimming
pools. "Residents Only," the signs on the wooden
fences warned. The cars in the underground garages
were Saabs and BMWs. Once Earl had brought
Frankie to show him the cars and the pool, but a guard
had chased them. When they were far enough away,
Earl had thrown rocks at him. Did he think Earl
wanted to swim in his stinking pool?

The harbor used to be lined with factories. He remembered sitting on the pier with Daddy when the
ships came in: freighters bringing sugar and car parts,
oil and rice and sheet metal. Daddy knew where they
were going, and he knew the men who worked in the
plants they were going to. They called to him on
the street or at the diner: "Hey, Johnny, that your
kid?"

The diner was around the corner from American
Chemical, only a block from their house. It never
closed, because the factories worked around the clock
and the men came in between shifts to eat. Nick and
his son Theo could fry eggs for a dozen men at a time,
with a side of ham or scrapple sizzling at the end of the

grill. And they always had something special for Earl: a cup of rice pudding, or a piece of custard pie.

"You got to get away from those babes, big boy," Nick would say. "Those babes can drive you crazy. I had six, so I know."

Earl nodded. Back home Angela would be squalling and Frankie would crawl around with his diaper hanging off. Mrs. Terwillis, who'd cared for the babies since Mama died, didn't mind their crying. She said all babies cried sometimes.

Daddy didn't mind the babies either. He'd sing to them right over their crying. Sometimes he'd hold them both, one in the crook of each arm, and do the polka. Then Frankie would laugh and Angela's little pink mouth would open in a round "O" of surprise.

But Earl was sure Daddy loved him most. Sometimes Daddy took him to the bar after supper. The TV on the shelf behind the bartender's head showed football or baseball, and the jukebox boomed. The air was thick with smoke. Men called to each other, laughing and shouting; their work boots thumped on the old tile floor. When Earl got tired, Daddy spread his jacket on the wooden bench that ran along the edge of the room, and Earl lay down and fell asleep. Late at night Daddy carried him home in his arms. Earl would wake up, gliding along the quiet streets, and see his father's face above him.

"Look at the stars, Earl," Daddy said, when he saw he was awake. "You can make a wish on them."

"I wish for candy," Earl murmured.

Daddy laughed and hugged him tight.

THIRTEEN

Addie wanted to look for Angela, too, but she was scared. Her family didn't usually go outside the wall: her mother's office was at home, and her dad worked for an insurance company next to Davis Market. Now and then they shopped at a suburban mall, or ate at a restaurant in Hopkins Square. A couple times a year they drove to a ball game at the stadium downtown. But Addie was most comfortable near home. The rest of the city seemed like a place where anything could happen, and where she did not belong.

She finished putting up the posters and went back to Maynard's list. Last night the two of them had interviewed the neighbors. On the day of the robbery, they'd had their air-conditioners on and their shades pulled down, so they hadn't seen or heard anyone. Addie was disappointed, but she didn't give up. The next thing on the list was searching the yard.

She did a really thorough job. She thought of the backyard as a square, with hedges on three sides and the house and a bit more grass on the fourth. She walked from one side to the other slowly, in straight lines, as if she were mowing. She looked everyplace she set her feet. She found a quarter, and her mom's silver earring, lost during a spring picnic. She found a Barbie shoe and a bit of ribbon and some cigarette filters left by old Mrs. Owen, who hadn't been able to give up smoking. But there was nothing else—until she went behind the hedge.

She nearly missed the clues, because they weren't obvious, and they took some thinking. The thinking was: thieves wouldn't walk straight into somebody's yard. They'd hide first, to see if anyone was home. What better place to hide than behind the hedge? They probably snuck the bikes out that way, too. Addie examined the dirt where there was a gap. Yes, here was a tire print in the dust, and another! So they *had* come this way!

She got down on her hands and knees, kept searching. She found part of a sneaker tread bigger than her own shoe, and a heel-print still larger—the second thief! The tracks were so muddled it was hard to tell them apart. Maynard had guessed there were three robbers, but she couldn't find a third set of prints. There was no point in looking in the yard—the only bare spot was under the swing set. But just to be on the safe side, she checked. And there, clear as day, was a track.

It was too small to be hers. Of course Maynard had been here, too; but his feet were larger, and he wore sandals with smooth soles.

She studied the footprint. The pattern was little squiggles instead of the geometric shapes found on older kids' shoes. Addie had that kind of sneakers herself when she was six or seven. She could picture them: zigzag on the side, tan soles, blue toe-caps, a wide Velcro closure. What were they called? She couldn't remember, but she felt sure the shoes were Angela's.

She tried calling Maynard, but no one answered. Still, for a while she felt excited. She'd found an important clue all by herself. Maynard was convinced that Angela hadn't been in Walnut Hill before he met her, but he must be wrong. What good luck that it hadn't rained, and wiped away the tracks. . . . I'll tell him first thing tomorrow, she promised herself.

She went to bed feeling tense. Late that night she woke abruptly. Images swirled in her mind, half-dream, half-real: the empty hutch, the footprint, a little girl's body with a blank where the face should be. What did Angela and her brothers want with Flag? Addie put her hands to her mouth. Once, in the pet store, she'd noticed a flyer that lingered in her memory. It was a photograph of a rabbit with eye sockets but no eyes. "Laboratories Test Cosmetics on Animals," the headline read.

Addie thought: What if they sold Flag to a laboratory? She tried to push the fear away, but it came back each time she closed her eyes.

Please, Flag, be strong . . . She clasped her hands, pictured the rabbit in her mind. *Wherever you are, whatever happens, don't give up. We're looking for you now, and we'll keep on until we find you, so don't give up.*

FOURTEEN

When Frankie and Angela knocked on Mr. Tiptop's door the next morning, bacon was already frying on the stove. Angela was happy. "Bacon starts with a B. I know some cusswords that start with B, too."

"Angela!" Frankie tried to shush her, but she wouldn't be quiet.

"One of them rhymes with 'witch,' and the other one sounds like busterd, only it's different." She tried to sneak a piece of cinnamon roll, but the old man must have heard, because his hand came out quick and stopped her.

"In this house we say grace before we eat, Angela."

"Do you like to cuss, Mr. Tiptop?"

"No, I don't *like* to cuss, but now and then I get aggravated. Then I can't help myself." Mr. Tiptop drained the bacon. He got out a pitcher of orange juice and a carton of milk and put them on the table. The whole time Angela was watching him. Finally she asked, "What makes you aggravated? Is it because you can't see?"

"Angela!" Now Frankie was mad. "That's rude!"

"I just thought it might be, on account of if I walk around with my eyes shut, I bump into things. But I have a magic wand, and if you want, I could make a wish for you."

Frankie was surprised to see that Mr. Tiptop was smiling.

"I don't mind being blind. I did at first, but I'm used to it now. I know my way around this apartment and around the neighborhood. I can recognize people by their steps and their voices. If I'd gone deaf—if I'd lost music—that would be different."

"Then you'd cuss," Angela said. "Like Frankie. One day he said 'shit' before he even got out of bed."

Frankie turned red. "I didn't, either. You're lying!"

Angela just smiled.

After they'd eaten, while he was sitting on the couch drinking coffee, Mr. Tiptop asked about Lula. "Usually I hear her walk by my window on her way to the bus stop, but lately I haven't. I asked Mr. Kim when I went to buy milk. He said he hasn't seen her since Friday morning."

"Earl said not to tell," Frankie mumbled.

"He's right not to tell the world, but your dad needs to know. If you bring me his phone number, I'll call him."

"He doesn't have a phone."

"But the place he's living probably does."

"Oh." Frankie hadn't thought of that. "I'll ask Earl."

"If you bring it, we can call him tonight."

"Thanks. Come on, Angela!"

They ran down the block. Earl was just finishing up the Cheerios when they came in.

"Mr. Tiptop's going to call Daddy! All he needs is the number!"

Earl wasn't feeling good. He was groggy, and his stomach felt pinched. "Beat it," he said.

After a while he stood up. Angela was watching TV, and Frankie was in the basement. Earl called for him to come upstairs. "What's this about Mr. Tiptop?"

"He says he'll call Daddy if we have the number."

"What's he doing in our business?" Earl demanded. He thought: For all I know, he could call the police.

Frankie stared. "He wants to help."

"Tell him we don't want his help." Earl shoved his fists into his pockets and looked out the window.

"We do, too. He gave us bacon and cinnamon rolls." Angela frowned at Earl. "That's better than what you bought."

"Shut up."

"Why can't he?"

"I don't know the number myself."

"Maybe you can find it. Then we'll call him together. It'll be fun."

"I'll think about it," Earl said.

Earl did think about it. He knew he was going to have to do something, and soon. That morning, before the little kids got up, he'd run all the way to the laundry and asked if Lula was there. The woman at the front desk telephoned Lula's floor.

"No one's seen Mrs. Bonner since Friday. She hasn't called in . . ." She looked at Earl kindly, but he left before she could ask questions. He felt panic. The money was almost gone, and the only things left to eat were two boxes of macaroni, three eggs, some peanut butter, and half a loaf of bread. Mr. Tiptop had fed the little kids. Earl knew he should be grateful, but instead he felt angry.

On the other hand, maybe *he* could call Daddy. Why hadn't he thought of that? There were the letters under his pillow, and notes that came with the weekly checks Daddy sent Lula. He started reading. In one of the early letters, he struck gold:

In an emergency you can call me in the early morning or evening. The phone number is 312-555-1750.

Earl stood there holding the letter. He felt like crying. What he needed had been there all along, but he'd been too stupid to look for it. He went back into the living room. "I found Daddy's number," he told the others.

"I want to talk to Daddy!" "*I* want to!" Frankie and Angela were shouting, but the shouting didn't bother Earl. He almost went to the pay phone on the corner right then. But he remembered the letter said to call in the early morning or evening, so they'd have to wait.

Frankie waited downstairs, near Spot. He lay spread-eagled on the cool floor, thinking. Last night he'd heard her scrabbling against the bricks, trying to escape. If she did, Angela and Earl would find out. He knew they wouldn't hurt her; but now and then Wayne dropped by. Frankie couldn't forget how he had hit her that first day. What if he came into the house and saw her? Would he squeeze her neck with his long, thin fingers?

There was another problem, too: Spot was hungry. The bag of wilted carrots was empty now. This morning Frankie had picked some weeds and stuck them under the bed; the rabbit sniffed them politely and turned away. Then he remembered the dollar Earl had given him. He found his old shorts in the dirty clothes and felt inside the pocket. The money was still there! He snuck over to Mr. Kim's. The store was out of carrots, so he bought a cabbage, brought it back, and gave it to her. For a while he hung upside down on his bed, watching Spot eat. He noticed that the pen was starting to smell. He scooped up the dark pellets and flushed them down the toilet. Then he found a bottle of cologne in Lula's room and sprinkled some around the bed. He sighed and lay back down.

Then, while he was resting, a picture came into his mind. He recognized the wooden cage in Spot's old yard: the bowls filled with food and water, fresh straw on the floor, and space to run around and play. Someone else had cared for Spot . . . Who was it? Frankie wondered. Was it a grown-up? An old man, like Mr. Tiptop? Or a kid, like him? He hung his head over the side and asked Spot; but she stared back from beside the cabbage with unblinking eyes.

Mr. Tiptop made his lunch. They talked about the old times, when Elvis was young. Mr. Tiptop described the moment he first heard Elvis sing. "I was hanging around the studio at lunchtime—it was right across the street from my shoe shop. He stepped up to the mike and did 'Cold River Blues.' I broke out in a sweat, 'cause there I was, hearing the greatest voice of the century right in my own hometown. If there was one thing in my life I wanted, Frankie, it was to sing with that boy.

"He knew I was a cobbler, 'cause I'd fixed his shoes up more than once, but he didn't laugh when I approached him. I told him shoes were my living, but music was my love. 'What part do you sing?' 'Bass,' I answered. He handed me the music to 'Blue Moon' and said, 'See what you can do.'

"When we cut that record, Frankie, it was near about the prettiest song ever made." Mr. Tiptop sat down at the piano and played it, singing softly. He sang the lead part first, then the bass. He sighed.

"Those times are gone, Frankie—they were gone before he even knew what they were doing to him. But I like to dream about them."

"I like to daydream, too." Frankie leaned over the keyboard. He closed his eyes and pictured Spot. "Sometimes I dream about having a pet." He knew he shouldn't have said the next thing, but he couldn't stop himself. "I saw the one I want when I was out with Earl and Wayne."

"What do you boys do when you go out?"

"Nothing much . . ." Frankie knew he wasn't supposed to talk about the bikes. On the other hand, Mr. Tiptop was his friend. Wayne had said, "Don't tell *Lula*. If you breathe a word to her, I'll cut your throat."

Frankie winced. "We go to other neighborhoods and look around."

"What for?"

"Nothing much . . ." Frankie looked at his feet. He wiggled his toes inside his old sneakers. "Except bikes."

"Bikes?"

"For the big boys. They never get me one."

"Where do the bikes come from?"

"People leave them in their yards . . ." Frankie tried to explain it the way they'd told him. "They're not good bikes. If they were good, they'd be locked up. And when Wayne and Earl are done with them, they take them back."

"Back where they got them?"

"That's what Wayne said." Frankie was confused about that. He'd been out looking, but they'd never taken him to return bikes.

Mr. Tiptop seemed to be thinking about that. "Earl seems like a good boy," he said softly.

"He is not—he's bossy. Wayne's mean, too. All he ever tells me is 'Shut up.'"

"Lula and Bucky left their mark on Wayne."

"What kind of mark?" Frankie thought of a birthmark, or the brand cowboys put on calves. He couldn't remember Wayne having anything like that. Mr. Tiptop didn't answer.

Then Frankie got an idea. It came from back when they'd been living with Beth-ann. One morning she'd got up and the folding chairs she kept beside her white marble steps were gone. "Somebody stole my chairs," Beth-ann fussed. "I'd like to catch that so-and-so. I'd put my foot right upside his head."

Frankie waited all day to see if she would catch him, but she didn't. Nobody ever brought those chairs back. Beth-ann had to go to Kmart and buy another set.

"Maybe Earl and Wayne stole those bikes," Frankie said.

"I want to talk to Earl," Mr. Tiptop said. "Today."

"I'll tell him." Suddenly Frankie felt scared. He got up and ran home quickly, without saying good-bye.

That night they tried to call Daddy. Earl gathered eighty cents in dimes and quarters. Then they went to the pay phone on the corner. Earl kept the door open so Frankie and Angela could hear. He punched the buttons: 312-555-1750. The operator's voice came on: "You have to dial a one before placing this call."

"Do I dial the one first?" Earl asked.

"Hang up and try again," the operator said. Earl realized she was a recording.

"I don't know whether to put the one before the area code or after," he told Frankie. His hands were shaking.

"Maybe before," Frankie said. He could tell Earl needed help.

"All right." Earl tried again. Another operator

came on. "Insert sixty cents for the first minute," she said.

Earl sorted through the change. He stuck in two quarters and a dime. The phone began to ring. It sounded very far away. It rang three times, four times. Then someone said, "Hello?"

"Daddy?" Earl said. "Is that you?"

"Who?" The voice was faint.

"Daddy?"

"You've got the wrong number," someone said.

Earl realized his mistake. "I want to talk to John—"

There was a click.

"I need to talk to John Foster," Earl said. He waited, but the phone was dead.

FIFTEEN

Addie showed Maynard the footprints.

"You were right, there were three robbers. And I think one was Angela. Take a look at this."

Maynard examined the track under the swing set. He measured it across and up and down, and made a drawing of it in his notebook. He did the same thing with the other prints. Then he went back to the smallest track, crouched down, and shook his head.

"I don't think it's hers," he said quietly.

"How come?"

"Angela had on rubber sandals." He flipped through the pages of his notebook, showed Addie the description he'd written down. "These are prints from a pair of sneakers. See the rim around the edge—right here? Those sandals wouldn't have that, 'cause their soles are flat."

"So what? She wore a different pair of shoes, that's all."

Maynard thought of the people he'd seen in the neighborhood past Grover Park. Some were nice, and had tried to help him. But even they had been shabby and worn-looking, like the houses they lived in. They didn't seem like people with money for extra shoes.

"I don't know about that," he said slowly. He told Addie about his search for Angela, and showed her the map, with the route he'd taken marked in red. He read what he'd written in his notebook, too. Addie got scared when he told about the boys who tried to steal his scooter. "You should have given it to them," she said. "My parents say: if someone tries to rob you, give them what they want. You can always buy another scooter."

"It wasn't just the scooter," Maynard said. "I have to be able to take care of myself, so I can go places and explore." He thought of Angela, who wasn't afraid to go anywhere.

"If you got beat up, I'd feel awful," Addie said.

"You would?" Maynard felt the blood rise to his face.

. . .

There were only a few responses to the notice Maynard had left on the Internet city page: one from a
downtown pet store with rabbits for sale; another
from an animal rights group, giving the phone numbers of the pound and animal shelter. Addie called
both places right away, but no one had turned in a
rabbit that looked like Flag. Hanging up, she noticed
the light that meant someone had left a message while
she was on the phone. Maynard showed her how to
play it back. A woman spoke, her voice distant and
polite: "Dr. Glenn, this is Mrs. Ponce from the Special
Office for Minors at Social Services, letting you know
we can't locate the children you reported on Saturday.
The only notation we have for that family is out of
date. If you want to call back, my number is 555-5623."

"What's that about?" Addie asked.

Maynard shrugged. His dad often got messages fol-
lowing up on his work at the hospital. But this one
mentioned Saturday. He thought back to the conversation in the garden: *"I can't imagine a man who'd
leave three children alone all weekend. I called Social Services . . ."*

"Play that again," he told Addie. "I've got a feeling
it's about Angela."

. . .

The thing he did next made Maynard uneasy, but he didn't see any way around it. He dialed Mrs. Ponce and made his voice as deep as possible.

"This is Dr. Glenn, returning your call about the children . . ."

"Yes, we couldn't find their current address. The last thing we have is from a while ago, from the emergency benefits division. They interviewed a John Foster, widower, with three children—Earl, Frank, and Angela. He was applying for money to stop a foreclosure on his home at 112 West Fait Street . . ."

"One-twelve West Fait Street," Maynard repeated. Addie scribbled the address in his notebook.

"We weren't able to help them. There are so many emergencies, and we have to be selective about who gets the funds . . ."

"You've been a big help. Good-bye." He hung up the phone, went straight to the computer, and opened the geography program. He plugged in the address, and the computer printed a map for him. Fait Street was in the oldest section of the city, near the docks.

"Maybe someone remembers them, and knows where they are," he told Addie. "I'll go down there and ask."

"This time I'm coming too."

"Good. We can leave early tomorrow morning. In the meantime, I'll check the bus routes."

"I've never taken the bus before." Addie felt nervous. But she thought of the footprint under the swing set. Was it Angela's? Was she sitting in a room in a house somewhere among the thousands of houses in the city, holding Flag? "If we have to walk the whole way, that's okay with me."

Maynard nodded. "I'll meet you at the corner by the wall at nine o'clock."

"Nine o'clock," Addie repeated. Her heart was beating fast. She wondered if she would sleep at all.

SIXTEEN

"I'm going with Wayne," Earl told Angela and Frankie. "We'll be back in a couple of hours."

"I want to go," Angela whined. "I'm bored, and there's no lunch."

"I don't have lunch to give you," Earl said. He went out the door and let it slam behind him.

Wayne was in a bad mood. He hardly spoke to Earl as they went down the boulevard and cut through along the railroad tracks. There was a dump where the tracks crossed Patterson Highway, but Wayne wouldn't slow down to see if there was anything valuable.

"Are we going to get bikes?" Earl asked.

"Just follow me," Wayne said.

They followed the tracks. There were a couple of old refrigerators thrown on a vacant lot near Cain

Street. Wayne looked in the backs to see if they had motors, but the back panels wouldn't come off without a socket wrench. One of them didn't look too bad. Wayne opened it, closed it again.

"You could fit in here," he told Earl.

Earl didn't answer.

"Get in, see what it's like."

"I don't want to."

"What are you, chicken? Think I won't let you out?"

Earl just stood there with his mouth closed tight. He could feel a shiver at the back of his spine.

"Chicken." Wayne spit on the ground, shrugged. They went on.

They walked along the edge of a marsh. Mosquitoes buzzed around their faces. Earl saw the shells of old factories. He could tell from the broken windows and junky yards that they'd been abandoned for years. "They were mills," Wayne said unexpectedly. "They ran back in Grandma's time. Now the cloth's made overseas."

"Did Grandma work there?" Earl had heard she worked in a pickle plant until she died.

"They didn't want no Polacks." Wayne kicked a bottle onto the tracks.

"What about Bucky's mom?"

"She's just a hillbilly. Can't even read and write."

"Do you ever see her?"

"Hell, no." Wayne acted like the question was dumb. "She lives in West Virginia, on a hill. Bucky said she lives on greens and potatoes."

"Potatoes aren't that bad," Earl said. "I like mashed potatoes." He felt his stomach rumble.

"You should look in the Dumpster behind the Food Mart. They throw bags of them in there when they're old." Wayne tossed his head to get the hair out of his eyes. "I done that when I was little. 'Dumpster rats' they called us."

"How come you did that? I thought Bucky was working."

"On and off. He didn't always live with us, either. This ain't the first time Ma and Bucky split up."

"Did Lula know? About the Dumpster, I mean."

Wayne laughed hoarsely. "Did she *know*? She was the one put me in there. I had to throw her what looked good." They walked farther. Wayne asked, "Has Ma been by?"

Earl shook his head.

"I hope she ain't drunk herself to death," Wayne said.

．　．　．

Just past the superhighway they turned off the tracks onto a road. It ran to a row of houses, all new, with a wooden sign out front: "Governor's Harbor." The marsh water had been drained into a creek that ran in front of the houses, and the sidewalks were wood, like docks. Earl saw that behind the first row of houses stood another; and behind it were more rows, though the fronts of some of them looked like foil. "Siding ain't on yet," Wayne explained. "They'll bolt it on. Cheap as hell. Bucky says these suburbs won't last twenty years."

"Who lives out here?"

"Mosquitoes mainly, and secretaries. Maybe some nurses too."

"They wouldn't have bikes, would they?"

"Who knows? Let's start looking."

The backyards were fenced, but these fences were only four feet high, so that Earl could see over them. But there wasn't much *to* see: Weber grills, plastic chairs and tables, here and there a baby's wading pool. Earl realized suddenly: "There's no place to ride a bike. Just the road in, and that comes off the superhighway."

"They're indoors, in the basements," Wayne said. "Want to bet?"

Earl didn't answer. Wayne looked around, vaulted over someone's fence, and peered into the low windows. "Laundry room is all you can see from here."

"Let's keep going," Earl said.

They didn't find anything in the yards, but inside an unfinished house, next to a pile of Sheetrock and 2 × 4's, was a red metal case filled with tools. Wayne was overjoyed. He closed it quickly and backed out, running to the trees at the edge of the construction site. Earl could tell from the way he ran that the case was heavy. Earl lurked behind the house a moment longer, as Wayne had told him to. Then he walked quickly down the road toward the entrance of the development. From beside the sign he could see Wayne behind a tree, the toolbox just visible beside him. Wayne waved with his hand for Earl to walk farther, and Earl did, his heart pounding in his chest. What if Wayne ran off? Earl didn't even know where he was.

But Wayne didn't run off. When Earl got to the place where the railroad tracks met the road, he stopped. A minute later Wayne came out of the woods.

"Not a bad haul, hey, Earl? Only the thing's so heavy, it's breaking my arm."

"I'll carry it," Earl said. But it *was* heavy. After a while Earl's shoulder felt like it was out of joint, and his leg hurt from the toolbox banging into it. He had to stop and put it down.

"You're a wimp," Wayne said. He picked up the case and they went on.

They left the railroad tracks at the underpass. Earl climbed up the bank and took the case from Wayne, who scrambled up beside him. Earl turned, still lugging the toolbox. Wayne grabbed his shoulder: "Hold on." He nodded toward a bare space below the underpass. Earl saw a couple of mattresses, like before, and a burned place on the ground where there had been a fire. "Let me check it out," Wayne said.

"We got the tools. Come on, man."

"Shut up," Wayne snapped.

This time Earl didn't have to stand guard, because there wasn't any road nearby, no one to see what Wayne would do. Wayne poked around the camp, emptying out a bag of clothes and old shoes. He kicked a pile of blankets off a mattress, turned it over, then did the same to the one beside it. He bent over, then screamed out loud, "Thirty dollars! It was under the mattress! Earl, look! Thirty dollars!" He waved the money in the air.

"Come on, Wayne, let's get out of here." Earl didn't know if his trembling was fear or excitement. He began to run, the heavy tool case banging against his leg. Wayne ran beside him, cuffing him on the shoulder with his fist: "How 'bout it, huh, Earl? What a day! And wait till we get to the pawnshop with them tools. That's the one thing he can sell no matter what. I heard him say so."

Wayne had a good story about the toolbox. Earl didn't go in, but the door was open, so he heard the whole thing. "My old man's in the hospital over Johns Hopkins, he got an infection in the bone from a cut he got in the bus barn. He told me to bring this stuff down and see what I could get for it."

The pawnbroker went through the box one piece at a time. "These are carpenter's tools," he said.

"They're from his old job."

"In good shape," the man muttered. "I'll give you eighty for all of it. You got to tell me your name and address, you know."

"No sweat." Wayne made something up. Earl saw the man hand him four twenties. Wayne came out the door looking sad, then as soon as he got around the corner he threw back his head and howled. He handed Earl forty dollars. "Don't say I never did nothing for you, punk."

"Thanks." Earl stuck the money deep in his pocket.

"I got more ideas." Wayne was jabbering away.

"What?"

"I know another place where the bums hang, down near the Federal Building. The cops want people to run them off 'cause they bother the tourists. Not only that, there's an old guy over near Lula's, he gets two kinds of Social Security 'cause he's blind. If we got in there, he couldn't even see to tell the cops."

"I gotta go," Earl said.

"If your check gets stolen, you get it back the next week," Wayne said. "Just file a claim. Works out good all around."

"I never heard of anybody like that over my way," Earl said. His mouth was dry.

"He's there, though. Lives in a basement, by a shoe repair."

"I'll see you later," Earl said. His stomach felt like he'd swallowed a hardball. He ran home, one hand in his pocket, clutching the money.

The first thing he did was take Frankie and Angela to the Food Mart. He bought them each two hotdogs and cartons of chocolate milk. Then he did the shopping: milk, Cheerios, lunchmeat, cheese, bread, orange juice, hamburger patties. That came to seventeen dollars. Angela begged for Gummi Worms; Earl bought her some, and a bag of suckers to use as bribes when she wouldn't act right. He bought himself a Coke Slurpee and a bottle of Pepto-Bismol. "Still got nineteen bucks," he couldn't help telling Frankie.

"Did you all get bikes?" Frankie asked. There was something different in his expression, something that made Earl's face, which had been smiling and open, close up.

"This has nothing to do with bikes. You don't know anything, Fat Frankie."

Frankie held his ground. "It used to do with bikes. If it don't now, how would I know?"

"Shut up!"

But Frankie was on to something else. He pulled on Earl's arm. When Earl pushed him away, he dug in his heels. Earl could see his stubborns coming on. "You got Angela Gummi Worms," Frankie said. "Now get me something."

"What?"

"Carrots." He had a funny look on his face.

"Carrots? What are you, nuts?"

"I'm hungry for carrots." Frankie's mouth was set in a line.

"For God's sake, Frankie!" Earl wasn't sure why he was so disgusted. He went into the store and bought a bag of carrots. He shoved them hard at Frankie: "Here!"

That evening Frankie got the mail. Usually that was Lula's job and they weren't supposed to touch it, but Frankie noticed that the mailbox was so jammed with papers nothing else would fit inside. He carried them downstairs and went through them one by one. Most were advertisements; others, with cellophane windows, Frankie guessed were bills. One was hand-written. Frankie thought he recognized Daddy's writing. He opened the envelope and found a photograph of a small white house, the kind that little kids draw, with a window on each side of the door. There was a tree, too, with a wooden swing hanging down, and behind that, a yard with a fence around it. It looked like flowers were poking over the fence.

There was also a check in the envelope. Frankie had seen checks before: he put his finger on the long line and thought he could read "Lula." Where the numbers went it said "85." And at the top, printed in black, was Daddy's name. Frankie knew the check was no good to anyone but Lula, and Lula was gone. That meant he could have it. He put it in the pocket of his shorts. "I'm rich," he told Spot. "Daddy sent me a check." He got up off the floor and did a little dance, to show how happy he was.

The last thing was a letter. Frankie couldn't read any of it. He folded it and stuck it under his pillow, the way Earl did. Then he looked out the window and saw Mr. Tiptop's shoes.

"Oh!" Frankie said. He put Spot back in her pen and ran upstairs. Mr. Tiptop had never come to Lula's before. Frankie was about to open the door when Earl grabbed his arm.

"Who's that?"

"Mr. Tiptop. I forgot, he wants to talk to you."

"What about?"

"Uh . . ." Frankie didn't want to say he'd told about the bikes. He turned red. Earl guessed it was something bad.

"Don't open it."

"But he—"

"I said, don't!" Earl's hand was in a fist.

Mr. Tiptop knocked, but no one answered. Angela was in the kitchen and didn't hear. Frankie just stood there feeling bad. He heard the old man call, "Frankie? Earl? Angela? Are you all right?"

There was silence. Mr. Tiptop knocked harder. "I'm worried about you. I want to make sure you're all right."

Earl looked at Frankie, and Frankie looked away.

SEVENTEEN

On the way to the corner, Addie almost changed her mind. That morning she'd seen a newspaper headline about tourists who were robbed by a gang right in front of City Hall. She stopped, looked back. She could see the corner of her house, the top limbs of the tree in her front yard. What she would give to be sitting under that tree right now, with her rabbit in her lap . . . But that was just a daydream. She started walking fast, kept her eyes forward. Maynard was standing on the corner, looking in his notebook. She called to him, and he looked up and smiled.

The bus stop was beyond the wall, down the hill near the drugstore. They had to wait for half an hour. Addie's nervousness soon became plain old discomfort: the sidewalk was sweltering. Inside the bus was even worse. She'd never been crammed in with so many people in her whole life. They smelled like sweat and dirty clothes. She ended up sitting next to a fat woman with a crying baby. She kept craning her neck to look at Maynard, who was perched on a bench beside an Asian teenager, studying his map. She saw the other boy look at it too and show Maynard something. The baby screeched. Addie tried making funny faces at it. It looked surprised, but it was so caught up in its crying that it couldn't stop. "Gas," the mother muttered sadly.

"Oh." Addie nodded, though she didn't know what that meant; but a moment later the woman glanced at her and smiled like they were friends.

Then, after what seemed like hours, Maynard pulled the cord, the bus squealed to a stop, and they got off. The air outside was hot and sticky, like a bowl of soup. There were no trees for shade, only row-houses piled so close they reminded Addie of bodies pressed against each other, sweating and steaming. She wiped her face with the sleeve of her T-shirt. "Are you sure we're in the right spot?"

"Pretty sure." There was a battered bench at the end of the block. They sat down there and studied the map. Maynard checked the street signs: "This is Patterson, and Boston's there, so Fait'll be that way."

"I'll just rest a minute," Addie said. She looked around. Children were jumping rope together on the wide, white sidewalk. To her surprise they looked a lot like kids on the playground in Walnut Hill. An older girl, blond like Addie and thick across the middle, sat fanning herself on the doorstep of a nearby house. She called to the others in a gravelly voice: "It's Tommy's turn, Megan. Show him how to do double Dutch, okay?"

"I wonder why they don't stay inside, in the air-conditioning," Addie murmured; but then she realized the windows and doors of the houses were open. Only some of the third-floor windows had fans whirring, pushing the heavy air back onto the street. If she were home, she'd put on her bathing suit and head straight for the pool. But beside her on the bench, Maynard wasn't sweating at all. His thin brown legs swung back and forth as if he had plenty of zip. *Zip* . . . the word echoed in her mind like the chants of the children jumping rope. He folded the map and got up.

"Ready to go?"

She nodded.

They walked to the corner, turned left, passing a diner that smelled like meat loaf and gravy. On the far side of the street were massive old buildings, and past them, beyond their cement piers, the water. "There's a tugboat!" Addie pointed. She couldn't help stopping to look. When she was four, *Little Toot* had been her favorite book.

"What was yours?" she asked Maynard.

"I loved Dr. Seuss. To tell you the truth, I still have all his books." He started reciting verses from *Green Eggs and Ham*. Addie remembered them and joined in. Just as they got to the "I do not like them" part, Maynard turned right. "It's here," he said suddenly. "Right here."

The place was nondescript, a narrow brick rowhouse with a few religious statues on the broad sill of the basement window. Maynard rang the bell. The door opened, first a crack, then wider. A gray-haired woman peeked out: "No English. Russian . . ."

"Do you know a family named Foster?"

"No English," she repeated. "My son speak."

"Is he home?"

"Taxi driver." She shook her head. "Come tonight."

"But we can't come tonight! You see, we took the bus all this way, and we're looking for my rabbit! And if you know about them, we can . . ."

The woman's eyes opened wide, as if she were

alarmed, and she closed the door. Maynard rang the bell, but nothing happened.

Addie felt like crying; then she did cry, quietly, right there on the steps. Maynard touched her shoulder. "Don't give up," he said. "There's still the neighbors."

But at the house to the right, no one answered. Maynard climbed the steps to 114, but before his hand hit the wood panel the door opened on its own. An empty stroller was thrust out, and a woman with a mountain of bleached hair came afterwards, a baby under one arm. "Oh," she said, noticing that the stroller had almost knocked Maynard off the steps. "Sorry about that." Then she saw Addie. "Mercy, hon, what's wrong with you?"

"We . . . we . . ." Addie swallowed, but Maynard jumped in: "We're looking for a family—Earl and Frankie and Angela Foster."

"Johnny's kids?" The woman's eyes were crinkly with wrinkles. "What do you want with them?"

"Angela's my friend," Maynard said.

"And you came down here in this heat . . . you must want to see her bad. But you're out of luck. Hon, those kids haven't lived 'round here since Johnny lost the house. They moved in with Beth-ann. Last I

talked to them, they were looking for another place—
her landlord didn't want no kids."

"Do you know where they went?"

"Sure don't—I've been wondering where they
ended up. It like to killed Johnny when they put that
place on the auction block. If you ask me, there ought
to be a law against banks that take back a house when
the owner's laid off. And him with them three
kids . . ." She shook her head, kissed the baby. "This
here Ralphie ain't mine—belongs to the lady up the
block. That's how it was with Johnny—I took care of
Angela and Frank when the two of them were so little they fit together in the same crib. I sure would like
to see them."

"When I saw Angela, the kids were staying with
Aunt Lula."

The woman was quiet for a moment. Maynard got
the feeling she was thinking things she didn't want to
say out loud. Finally he asked, "Do you remember her
last name? Is it Foster?"

"Lord no, hon. She was married to a great big hillbilly. Both of them could really tie one on—what the
heck was he called? Bucky Bonner, I think."

"Bucky Bonner." Maynard looked at Addie. "So
Lula would be Lula Bonner?"

"That's right, Lula Bonner. And if you find her, or if you see them kids, tell them Helen Terwillis sends her love. And give Angela a kiss for me."

"I will!" Maynard said, and then, realizing what he'd promised—"I won't! I mean, I don't kiss girls."

"Just wait a couple years, then do it." The woman winked and waved. Maynard and Addie headed up the street.

"Let's look her up in the phone book!" Suddenly Addie didn't mind the heat. "We can go there now."

Maynard pointed to a dark cloud above the harbor. Before his hand came down, fat raindrops started exploding on the sidewalk. They hurried toward the bus stop. Maynard zipped ahead, then turned and waited. That's when Addie remembered.

"Zips!" she said. "That's what they're called."

"What?"

"Those sneakers. The ones that made the tracks under the swing set. They're Zips."

Before Maynard could answer, thunder rumbled.

EIGHTEEN

There was no Lula Bonner in the phone book. That night Maynard looked twice, with Addie peering over his shoulder. There was a Frank Bonner, and a George and a Bernard. "That could be Bucky," he said, putting his finger on the address. "Let's find out where he lives."

He underlined 2206 Whiteford Avenue, then typed the address into the computer. The map showed a street west of Grover Park. "They might both live there . . . but Angela never talked about her uncle, at least not that uncle." Maynard wasn't going to mention Mr. Rogers, not right now. "Let's call him."

A gruff, unpleasant man answered the phone. "Lula doesn't live here, never has. Me and her split up last year."

"Could you tell us where to find her?"

"Let me guess—she owes you money." His laugh was hoarse.

"No, we have something to give her."

The man made a crude remark. Maynard held tight to the receiver, tried again. "It's something valuable for her and her husband," he said carefully. "But she's the one who has to sign for it."

He laughed again. "For her and me, huh?"

Maynard waited.

"It's 315 Hoyer," he mumbled then. Maynard repeated the address, and Addie wrote it in the notebook. He hung up. Outside the rain was coming down in sheets.

"You know what's weird?" Maynard's eyes had that intense look, like they were seeing things beneath the surface of their skins. "I've been on that block. I was there the first time I went looking for Angela."

"What's it like?"

He didn't want to scare Addie, but he couldn't lie, either. "Some of the houses were boarded up, and the rest look pretty bad . . ."

"Can we take the bus?"

"Probably not. It's only a few miles."

"A few miles," Addie said weakly. Her legs already ached from today. But she thought of Flag: Was she hungry? Had someone brought her water? Did the thieves know rabbits die in too much heat?

"I'll call you as soon as I get up, okay?"

He nodded, already thinking of what route they'd take, and what he'd say to Angela once he found her.

NINETEEN

If you'd asked Angela to describe the worst day in her life, she might have told you about the time she didn't get a Blueberry Muffin doll for her birthday, or the morning Missy Price shook her arm so hard Angela let go of the quarter she was clutching and it rolled down the sidewalk into the storm drain. Those were bad days—very bad. But this was even worse.

And it was Frankie's fault. He got mad when she put on the sweatshirt she'd worn to the park before—the one Maynard said was his. "Where'd you get that?" he'd yelled.

"Off the floor." Angela was surprised. Frankie never cared what anyone wore.

"That's mine," he shouted. "You can't have it."

"Says who?"

"Says me!" And he'd grabbed it and yanked till it

came off over Angela's head. Then he rolled it in a ball and threw it in the closet, as if it were poison.

He wouldn't go to Mr. Tiptop's, either. He mumbled something about bikes, and Earl not opening the door. Angela wanted bacon and pancakes, but she felt funny going on her own. Finally she got a jar of grape jelly and a spoon and sat in front of the TV. *Sesame Street* was on. They were teaching W. Angela knew all the mystery words: "win," "whoops," "wow," and "wonder." Then she read the mystery sentence: "Will Wally wave the wonderful wand?" She clapped for herself, since there was no one else to clap for her. But she forgot about the spoonful of jelly in her left hand. It flew across the room and splattered on the wall. She cleaned up the mess the best she could, using the bottom of her shirt. At first she didn't like the purple smear the jelly made, but when she scrubbed at it the stain spread out, so that it looked like a pale pink cloud. I'm floating on a cloud, Angela thought. I'll float to the park and play with the big kids there.

She ran outside. The air was thick and warm, like a gritty blanket; the people sitting on their steps fanned themselves slowly, and barely nodded as Angela went by. Kids in the park were playing statues. Angela watched a boy land and stay still. Sweat was pouring off his face. After a little while his leg shifted. "He moved!" Angela shouted. "Look at him! He moved!" The boy glared. Angela came closer, hoping they'd ask her to play. A girl was swung so hard she bumped Angela's legs. "You stink," she said.

"I don't," Angela answered, but right away the others took up the chant: "You stink!" They held their noses. The boy who'd glared at her danced around, singing, "Peeeeee-yoooooo!" Angela stomped her foot to make him stop. "I'm a princess!" she shouted. "If you don't behave, I'll have your heads chopped off."

The kids stared at her for a split second, and Angela stood up straight and tall. Then someone muttered, "Princess Stinky." The others began giggling. Some of them howled with laughter. "Shut up!" Angela screamed. She rushed at a girl and tried to scratch her face. The others pulled her off and flung her down. She got up and tried again; this time three kids grabbed her arms and legs and swung her high in the air. They let go. She landed—whump—on her backside on the hard ground. "So long, Princess Stinky!" someone called, and they ambled away.

Angela lay still. Her whole body hurt, and the center thong of her sandal had come loose from the sole, so that it dangled off her foot. A tiny parade of ants marched past her nose, then turned toward her, as if they sensed she couldn't get up. Their leader stopped six inches from her face. He stood up and waved his front legs at her, as if he were conducting an orchestra. Angela screamed. She jumped up and limped away. Tears leaked down her cheeks, and she scrubbed at them furiously. "I'll fix those kids good," she sniffed; but she knew there were too many of them and they were too big.

She left the park, carrying the broken sandal in one hand. She watched the sidewalk for broken glass and dog mess, keeping her head low so no one would see she'd been crying. Once she turned and stuck her tongue out at the park, but nobody saw, and it didn't make her feel any better.

She walked uphill. Far off, through the haze, she could see the stone wall by Maynard's neighborhood, and she thought of visiting him there. But the hot asphalt stung her foot. Just then the door of the air-conditioned drugstore swung open. The blast of air cooled Angela's face. She grabbed the door before it closed and slid inside.

She'd never been to the drugstore by herself. When

she came with her aunt, Lula was usually in a hurry, and she pulled Angela along so that she didn't have a chance to look at her favorite things. Today, Angela thought, I can take my time. She decided to start in the hair section.

It was wonderful: there were barrettes and twistees and brushes and hairbands and bows; all colors, but the best were pink, purple, and aqua. Velvet ribbons and gold and jewel-studded hairclips hung from a metal rack. Angela touched each package. Sometimes she took one down, examined it, and carefully put it back in the right spot. What would a red barrette look like in her own brown hair? She ran her fingers through it hurriedly, suddenly aware that it had not been brushed. There . . . that was better. She used to wish she was blond, like Barbie, but Beth-ann said blond was nothing but a pain. "Miss Clairol costs a fortune, and it don't look natural, anyway," she'd said when they were alone. "I'll tell you, honey, stick with what you got." She'd made Angela a ponytail, the kind that arched up high, and tied it with a pretty bow. Angela sighed. She took down a tube of hair mousse, looked it over, put it back. She wondered who owned the store. Was it a lady? Was she pretty? Did she come at night, when it was closed, and take whatever she wanted? Behind her someone coughed. She turned and saw a woman in a uniform. The words Rite Aid were printed in black over the pocket. "Oh." Angela blushed. She hadn't realized anyone was watching.

"You can't stay here without a grown-up," the clerk said.

"I'm just looking."

"You can't."

"My brothers do. They come to see the candy."

"Maybe they've got money."

"I do, too." Angela stuck her chin out. "Six thousand dollars, from the lotto jackpot. It's at home, in my dresser drawer." She edged toward the door, her broken sandal in her hand. "I'll come back and get whatever I like."

The clerk didn't bother to answer. She watched as Angela went out onto the hot sidewalk. When Angela looked back, she was still standing in the doorway with her arms across her chest.

"Meanie," Angela said, but she didn't try to get back in. She trudged across the street and headed home.

Then, finally, something good happened, because when she came around the corner Mr. Tiptop's door was open! She hurried in, calling, "It's Angela! I'm here, Mr. Tiptop!"

A stranger came out of the bedroom, carrying an armload of clothes. She was wearing a housedress shaped like a tent, and the loose skin under her chin bobbled so that she reminded Angela of a big old turkey. Her tone was accusing: "You're one of those kids from around the corner, aren't you?"

"I'm not, either." Angela took a step backwards.

"I'm Al's sister." The woman shook her finger. "I told him to report you kids to the police, but he's afraid they'll split you up. He's too kindhearted for his own good." She shoved a dust mop around the edge of the room, then shook it near Angela's face. "Why he stays here is beyond me: crime and drugs, and you nasty kids . . ."

"We aren't nasty, either."

"You ate up all the groceries, and I bet you took his spare change, too."

"We did not!" Angela glared. "And he offered us that food. He said he liked eating with us."

The woman didn't believe her. "I'm giving you a message, child, but you don't get it."

"What?"

"You aren't welcome here no more."

Angela blinked. She couldn't believe her ears. "Not even Frankie?"

"Frankie . . . he's the fat one, isn't he?"

"He's not the only one who's fat." Angela should have kept her voice low, but she didn't. The stranger almost pushed her out the door.

She went home. She was tired, and her bare foot hurt from walking on the rough sidewalk. Earl was sitting on the stoop, his chin in his hands. "I told you not to leave without asking," he snapped.

Angela didn't bother to answer. She kept her head down.

"What's wrong?" Earl demanded. "Did something happen?"

"My shoe broke."

"That's no big deal. Those zorries only cost fifty cents."

She shrugged. She was about to sit by Earl when he said, "You smell like pee."

"I don't, either," Angela said, but she went into the house, slamming the door behind her.

She went straight to the bathroom. There was a washcloth on the hook by the shower. She held it under the faucet, then smeared it with soap. She took off her clothes and washed herself so hard she turned red all over. She went downstairs to find clean clothes, but after she'd only been there a minute she heard something that sounded like claws. She screamed and ran. Frankie was sitting by the TV.

"What's wrong?"

"There's something under your bed!"

"I'll go check," he said.

A little while later he came back. "There's nothing there, Angela. If you come down, I'll show you."

There wasn't anything—no monsters, and no signs of them. Angela checked under the bed twice. The floor there smelled sickly sweet, like perfume. The closet was the usual bunch of mismatched shoes and wadded clothing. There was nothing different in the bureau drawers, or behind them. Angela dropped the towel she'd wrapped around her and put on underwear and a dress. She hurried upstairs so she wouldn't be alone.

The boys were watching cartoons. As soon as she sat down, the show was interrupted for a White House press conference. Pretty soon Angela started to hate President Clinton. She stretched two fingers out like scissors and pretended to cut his hair. Then she pretended to cut off his head.

"If I was President, I'd give every kid a store," she said.

"What kind of store?"

"A big one, with toys and pretty clothes and hair stuff and kittens and a restaurant like McDonald's."

"And rabbits," Frankie said. "They're my favorites now."

"And track shoes, and brand-new bikes, and a money machine if you needed it." Earl stretched his legs across the space between the couch and the TV. Most of his socks showed beneath the cuffs of his worn jeans.

"And it would be just for us," Angela said. "If a grown-up wanted something, we'd say no." She thought of the clerk in the drugstore. "We wouldn't even let them look."

"What if they needed food?"

"Tough," Angela said, but Frankie thought that was too mean. "They could have leftovers," he said.

"They'd have to say please and thank you."

"What if they didn't?"

But Angela didn't answer, because someone was pounding on the door. Earl looked out the window. "It's Wayne," he said.

Frankie begged, "Don't let him in!"

"I have to—he saw me."

"Don't!"

Earl did anyway. Frankie went downstairs, and Angela did, too. "I don't like Wayne," she said. "He's got pimples."

Usually Frankie laughed when she said pimples, but this time he didn't. Angela saw that he was trembling. "Frankie, what's wrong?"

He shook his head and wouldn't answer.

That evening Angela went to bed early. Her stomach hurt from not eating. There was food in the kitchen, but she didn't feel like fixing it. Through the ceiling she heard the low rasp of Wayne's voice. She put her hands over her ears and pretended Beth-ann was there, singing her favorite song: *"You are my special angel . . ."* Out in the street a truck rolled by, shaking the basement walls. Angela opened her eyes and saw the magic wand lying in the dirty clothes beside the mattress. She picked it up and hugged it to her chest. *I wish for Daddy and Beth-ann,* she thought. Upstairs Wayne was arguing with Earl. Angela sighed. She pulled the sheet up over her head and tried to go to sleep.

TWENTY

Frankie wasn't sure what made him think of the coal bin, but he was glad he did, because it was the best hiding place in Lula's house. Earl and Angela didn't even know about it. There was probably only one other person who did. That person was Wayne.

It wasn't as if Wayne had been downstairs to the basement—usually he stayed on the front steps, talking to Earl. But since Lula left, he came by more and more, as if he wanted the house for himself. Once he strolled into the kitchen and opened the refrigerator door, as if the food there belonged to him. What if he wanted something in the basement? What if he went downstairs and saw Spot?

Frankie shivered. He stood on the top step, inside the basement door, listening to the big boys talk. If Wayne came close, if the doorknob turned, he would run down, grab Spot, and climb out the coal chute.

Wayne didn't come close. He and Earl were arguing about something. Their voices rose and fell in the front room. Finally Wayne said, "I'll see you tomorrow morning." He went out, slamming the door behind him.

For a while Frankie just stood there. He heard Earl turn down the TV and flop onto the couch. "Oh, man," Earl muttered. But Frankie didn't pay attention. All he could think was: Wayne's coming back tomorrow.

He gulped. Spot wasn't safe if Wayne was in the house. Maybe nothing would happen, maybe he wouldn't even go downstairs. But again Frankie remembered how Wayne hit her that first day. For all Wayne knew, Spot could have died. He hadn't even seemed to care.

Frankie didn't know what to do. Then, like a bird that flitted from place to place but finally lit, an idea came into his mind and stayed: run away.

That was best for Spot, too, because the coal bin was an awful place: dark and dirty and hot. The moment Frankie opened the lid, the rabbit was there, scrabbling to escape. Her fur was thick with grime, and she'd upset the cup of water Frankie had put in the corner. He picked her up and held her, but she twisted in his arms, kicking with her hind feet. He stroked her, then sang to her to calm her down. They'd go now, while Earl and Angela were sleeping. He stood still, unsure of what to take. Finally he got the bag of carrots from the kitchen. He stuck Spot under his shirt and tiptoed out the door.

It was very late: hardly any cars were on the streets. The last drops of a summer shower cooled his sweaty face. Frankie stayed close to the fronts of the rowhouses. He didn't believe in monsters, like Angela did, but he knew bad people came out at night: robbers and crack-heads. He scurried from one shadow to the next, trying to keep out of sight.

He tried to think of where to go. The park was four blocks up; but the only shelter there was benches, and he'd heard that homeless men took most of those. Downtown, to the south, was patrolled by private guards. He had no money but the check. He felt in his pocket—it was there, carefully folded. But it said Lula, not Frankie. He stopped. He knew, suddenly, who might cash that check, but he'd have to hide till morning to find out.

He went around the corner, to the alley. There was a garage connected to the back of Mr. Kim's, with a

Dumpster beside it. Frankie tried the double doors; they were padlocked, but the lid of the Dumpster moved under his hand. He swung it up and felt inside. The trash was mostly boxes, crushed flat and jammed against each other. Frankie pulled some out and piled them up to make a step. He scrambled up, cradling Spot against him, tipped himself inside, and pulled the lid down tight.

He woke abruptly. Spot was asleep, her paws stretched out against his neck; but outside someone cursed and banged the side of the Dumpster. The lid flew open, and a wall of cardboard smacked Frankie right in the face. "Hey!" He was so shocked he forgot that he was hiding. Spot scrambled under his T-shirt. "Cut that out!"

"So I found who did it . . ."

A girl's face peered over the metal edge. Frankie recognized Mr. Kim's daughter, Hang, but before he could jump up, her hand darted out and grabbed his wrist. "Why you make a mess with those boxes?" she hissed. "I had to clean that up." When she said clean, it sounded like "crean." Other kids teased her about the way she talked, and made her mean. "Let go . . ." Frankie struggled. Spot wiggled under his shirt.

"What you got on you—a rat?" Hang jumped back, but as soon as she saw Spot's ears, she grabbed him again. "Where you get that rabbit?"

"I found her in the alley." Frankie turned bright red. Hang stared at him.

"You can't lie for nothing, Frankie."

"I'm not lying—she's mine."

All Hang said was, "Get out."

She never let go. She marched Frankie into the store, which was closed because it was so early. Mr. Kim was making coffee in big silver pots. Hang spoke to him in another language—Korean, Frankie guessed. Her father looked at him kindly. "Why are you in the Dumpster?"

"I . . . I had to run away, because of Wayne." Frankie stared at the cracked linoleum floor. "I hid in the Dumpster because I wanted to ask if you would cash this check. It's for Aunt Lula, but she's gone." He took the folded paper from his pocket and held it out.

Mr. Kim examined it carefully.

"I can't cash it," he said finally. "It's hers."

"But she's gone."

Mr. Kim nodded slowly, his dark hair falling over his forehead. His face was scarred, as if he'd been through hard times, too. "Mr. Tiptop told me. You kids have food?"

"We got enough." Frankie thought Earl wouldn't want them taking stuff for free.

"Why you need the money, then?"

"I have to go somewhere."

"That's what the check is for—bus tickets." Mr. Kim pointed to a line in the bottom corner.

Suddenly he looked at Spot. "Where'd you get that rabbit?"

Frankie turned red all over again. "In the alley," he whispered. The storekeeper knew better.

"You kids been stealing things? That's what I see around here, kids taking stuff that isn't theirs! I know about Wayne, but I thought you three . . ."

Frankie didn't wait to hear the rest. By now Hang had eased her grip. He twisted free and bolted out the door.

There was an opening like a little hall between two houses partway down the block. Frankie hid there for a minute, trying to think of what to do. The check was no good, and Hang would tell the neighborhood kids about Spot. Frankie was afraid they would snatch her away. If only there were somewhere he could sit down and figure things out: where he was running to, and how to get there. . . . Suddenly, a place came to his mind. He looked around—the coast was clear. He clutched the rabbit to his chest, scurried out, and ran up the street as fast as he could.

TWENTY-ONE

"I know where he lives," Wayne said. "It's right around the corner."

Earl didn't answer. He was pissed off, and scared, too. His upper arm hurt where Wayne had grabbed it. And now Wayne was strolling along smoking as if nothing had happened.

"Want one?" He offered the pack.

"No." The last time Earl tried smoking, he'd sputtered like a wet match.

But Wayne was acting real concerned. "You're too uptight, Earl. You let those kids get on your nerves. What do you think you are, their mom?"

Earl shrugged.

"They'll get along. So Angela wanted to tell you something: it'll wait. I used to sit by Lula's bed when she was drunk, waiting for her to open her eyes, and if

I waited long enough, she did. It all works out in the long run."

They came to the steps of the corner store. Wayne opened the door. "I'll only be a second."

I ought to run, Earl thought. This is when I ought to run. But suppose he turns and looks through the door? I'm fast, but Wayne is faster.

His mind drifted. A few blocks east there was a spot where you could see down the hill, over the tops of the rowhouses, to a thin sliver of bay. What if he had his own boat, chugging along out there? Nothing bad could touch him out on the water. He'd stand on the foredeck and drink coffee, hear the gulls shrieking for scraps of fish.

Earl looked up suddenly. Wayne was standing on the next step up, staring at him. "He lives just up the street."

"Who?"

"The old blind guy, the one I told you about. Man, Earl, you're in dreamland."

"Yeah." Earl blushed.

"Let's go."

Earl pictured Mr. Tiptop cooking Frankie's breakfast. The old man was nicer than anybody ought to be.

Last Easter, after Daddy left, Frankie came skipping home with three chocolate eggs in a paper bag. They had names on them in sugar icing. Frankie and Angela ate theirs, but Earl had kept that stupid egg for weeks. When he looked at his name, Earl, something seemed to grab at him from the inside. He could almost hear the blind man singing—a sad song, soft and low.

"I don't need money," he said now. "I still got thirteen dollars from the other day."

"Thirteen bucks ain't going to last you two days, not feeding Fat Frankie and Angela."

"We can go downtown, to that free place. We're all right."

"Maybe so, but you're in this with me, and I'm not. I had to give Bucky twenty dollars. Wouldn't you know he blew most of it on beer? Got so bombed he threw up in the bathroom. I nearly puked myself, cleaning that mess up."

"Why'd you give him the money?"

"He didn't have nothing to eat." Wayne shrugged. "He asked 'Did I have any money?' What was I supposed to say?"

Earl got a sinking feeling. He didn't know what Wayne should have said. If it'd been him, wouldn't he have done the same thing?

182 ·

Wayne picked up on that. "Don't worry about the old man," he said. "I'm not going to hurt him, just scare him enough to get the check. And they'll give it back, once he reports it."

Earl's feet felt like lead.

"Hurry up, man."

"He fed Frankie and Angela."

"He's blind, man. He won't even know you're there."

TWENTY-TWO

Maynard turned before he climbed the steps to 315. They'd walked the whole way. Addie was full of doubts: What if her memory of the sweatshirt in the yard was wrong? What if everything they'd figured out was wrong? What if someone else had taken Flag?

On the other hand, what if they were right? What if the thieves were there, at Lula Bonner's house? Would they have guns? Would they shoot before they even knew who she and Maynard were? And why they'd come?

It was still early; the sidewalks smelled of last night's rain. Addie tried to calm down, but she couldn't. She felt like she was walking on the thin ice of a frozen pond. Any second it might give way. Then she would slide into the cold darkness and never be seen again.

Because both of them had lied about today. Addie told her mom she was hanging out with Maynard; they weren't sure what they'd do, maybe go to the pool or the deli. Mrs. Johnson was in a rush, preparing food for a wedding; she nodded, and didn't ask questions. Maynard's dad thought he was going to spend the day solving a mystery on the Internet. But when Dr. Glenn drove off, Maynard told the housekeeper he had to go next door. So nobody knew where they were. If something bad happened, their parents wouldn't even know where to look.

She asked Maynard about it. He didn't want to say so, but he'd also been thinking that the thieves might have a weapon. And what Addie said was true: they had no backup, since no one knew where they were going, or why. "If they'd known, they would have stopped us," Maynard said quietly.

"Would they have gone themselves?"

"I doubt it. You see, to someone on the outside, the whole thing seems far-fetched." He noticed that Addie had circles under her eyes, as if she hadn't slept. He wanted her with him, but not if she didn't want to be. "Do you want to go back?" he asked. "'Cause I can go by myself. I did before, you know."

"No. She's my rabbit, so I need to be there. If any-one should go back, it's you."

"I'm not going back! I want to know the truth. And find Flag, too," he added hastily. He took a deep breath, let it out. Then he thought of a way to make it safer. "But we'll have to find a phone, so I can leave a message."

"That looks like a store up there," Addie said. "We can go inside and ask."

It turned out there *was* a phone inside the store; the Asian man who seemed to be in charge pointed to the back, beside the freezers. Maynard threaded his way through crates of cabbages and potatoes. He dialed his dad's pager, leaving only the address on Hoyer Street. Then he thanked the man and went back out.

"It's in this block. There's 309, 311, 313 . . . it's that one, there."

They agreed Maynard would knock alone. That way, if there was trouble, Addie could run for help. Maynard raised his hand and let it fall. For a time it seemed no one was home. Then, slowly, the door swung open, and Angela appeared.

"Maynard!" she cried out. "You came!"

He was glad to see her, despite his fear. "Is anyone else here?"

"No. Frankie went somewhere, and Wayne woke Earl up and took him away. He left before I could tell him Frankie's gone. He called downstairs and told us not to go nowhere till he got back."

"So you're alone?"

She nodded, smiling. "I wished for Daddy and Beth-ann, but the wand sent you instead."

"My friend is with me—this is Addie."

Addie hadn't expected to like Angela, but looking into the girl's small, dirty face, she felt moved. How could someone leave a little child alone? But Maynard shifted restlessly from foot to foot. "Can we come in? We're looking for something, and we think it might be here." They went into the front room.

"What?"

"Addie's rabbit. It's missing from her yard. The person who took it was wearing special sneakers called Zips."

Addie was watching Angela's face. She didn't look like she was trying to hide anything. "It's not here," she said. "But Frankie's got Zips. They're old and smelly, 'cause they came from Earl. I like new shoes. For my birthday, I'm getting slippers made of solid gold."

"Does Frankie like rabbits?"

"Frankie likes all animals, but rabbits are his favorites. He said so last night."

Addie crouched down, so she was looking right into Angela's eyes. "Are you *sure* you haven't seen a rabbit, Angela? It's real, real important to me."

But Angela shook her head. "I didn't see one. I heard something, though, under Frankie's bed. It sounded like a monster."

"Could we look?"

"Sure, follow me."

But there wasn't much of anything under Frankie's bed—only some dried-up leaves, and an empty cereal bowl. The space reeked of perfume, as if someone had emptied a whole bottle on the floor. Addie thought she might smell something else, something familiar, but whatever it was, the perfume covered it up. She looked on the bureau, then among the bedcovers. Under the pillow was an envelope. "What's this?" she asked.

"I don't know . . ." Angela turned it over. "It's from Daddy—see, that's his name: John Foster. But I can't read cursive, so we'll have to wait till Earl gets home."

"I can read it for you," Addie said.

Dear Lula,

Good news! I've got a tenant house—here's a picture, so the kids'll know what to expect. Beth-ann will be here too—the beach is only a half-hour commute. I never thought we'd end up in the country, and I doubt that this is permanent. But I'm worried about Earl—he's old enough to wander. The city streets are not the place to be without your old man near.

And the farm's good: free milk and vegetables, animals for Frankie, lots of space to run and play. There's a swing out front for Angela, too.

Thanks so much for watching the kids. This check will cover their bus tickets. Please put them on the 5:00 p.m. Greyhound this Saturday afternoon. I'll pick them up at 9:30 in Tillington . . .

"Wait!" Angela didn't let Addie finish. She looked in the envelope, shook the letter, turned the picture over. "It isn't here!"

"What?"

"The check!" Her eyes filled up with tears. "Now we can't go, 'cause the money's gone! Frankie must have taken it!"

"Maybe he went to buy the tickets," Maynard said.

Angela shook her head. "He doesn't know what it says 'cause he can't read."

"Why'd he go, then?" Addie asked gently.

"He was afraid of Wayne."

"Who's Wayne?"

"He's my cousin. He's old, almost eighteen, and he's mean, too. Earl said . . ." Angela didn't like thinking of what Earl said. "He killed a cat," she blurted. "He choked it with his hands."

Addie felt a tremor pass through her. She took a deep breath and got up quickly, putting an arm around Angela's shoulders. "We'll get your dad to send another check, and we won't leave you here alone, either, in case Wayne comes. And in the meantime we'll search real hard, in case there's anything else that's hidden, like the letter."

"I'll search, too," Angela said.

It was Maynard who found it. He'd gone into the basement opposite the bedroom and looked behind the furnace. There was a pile of bricks there, neatly stacked; but no sign of Flag. He looked in the dry sink and the window wells. On the far side of the furnace was a wooden bin that extended to a window grating. He lifted the lid, put it back, lifted it again. In the far corner of the grimy box was an overturned cup. He picked it up. The wood underneath it was wet.

"Addie?"

She knew by the way he shouted to come fast.

"Look—this was spilled recently, otherwise it'd be dry. And here . . ." Carefully he plucked something from the rough wood on the edge of the bin. "It's hers, isn't it?"

Addie took the little tuft of fur and held it to her face. She closed her eyes. "If only we knew where he went."

Angela's face lit up. "I might know. I don't know why I didn't think of it before."

They stared at her.

"He's probably at Mr. Tiptop's," she said matter-of-factly. "He goes there a lot. Only I can't, 'cause the woman said I wasn't welcome anymore."

"We won't leave you here alone," Addie said.

"No. I'll go." Maynard stood up straight, looked hard at Addie. "Will you be okay?"

She nodded.

"I'll come back as fast as I can."

Angela told him where to go. Then she and Addie sat on the couch and talked. She told Addie about all the trips she'd taken: to China, Ireland, and Japan; and about the velvet gowns she'd worn, and the jewelry, too. That's when they heard noises on the outside steps. Someone knocked on the door.

Addie gasped, "Don't open it!"

"I have a way of peeking, to find out who it is."

"Are you sure they won't see you?"

Angela nodded. She ran upstairs. She came down giggling. "I can't believe it—it's Maynard's dad!"

Addie looked out the window, then she flung open the door.

"Lovely to see you, ladies," the fat man said. He was dressed in his green hospital suit, as if he'd left there fast. "This address appeared on my pager, and I called home, looking for my errant son, only to discover he was missing."

"He's not here," Angela said. "But he'll be back soon."

"May I ask you where he is?" Dr. Glenn sounded strained.

"He went to Mr. Tiptop's, looking for Frankie." Addie sighed. "I hope you're not too mad," she said. "We can explain."

"I told Maynard not to go back through Grover Park, under any circumstances."

"We went around it," Addie said weakly.

"Maynard has deceived me, and caused risk to himself and you."

She stepped forward then. "Please don't punish him, Dr. Glenn. You don't know what he's done."

"I certainly don't," Maynard's father answered. "But I want to—very much."

Addie said, "He's almost found Flag."

TWENTY-THREE

The blind man's door was closed. Wayne tried the knob, but it wouldn't turn. He knocked and stepped back. Earl stood behind him.

"Who is it?" A sliver of face appeared behind the chain bolt.

Wayne tried to disguise his voice. "I just want to ask a question."

"What about?"

"Frankie Foster." Wayne winked at Earl.

"Oh, Frankie . . ." The old man was suddenly silent, as if he sensed something might be wrong. "He's not here," he said loudly.

"Could we talk?"

Mr. Tiptop hesitated. Then he undid the chain and let them in.

•   •   •

Earl thought he knew at once he'd made a mistake. For one thing, Wayne stuck his foot against the door, so it couldn't be closed again. For another, Wayne couldn't think of what to say.

"What do you want with Frankie?"

The question hung in the dark, still air. Wayne's eyes were scanning the room, darting back and forth like minnows. Everything was shadowed. The smell of last night's dinner drifted like a cloud toward the open door.

"Where's the light switch?" Wayne asked.

"I know you, but I can't recall . . ."

"I'm here to get your check." Wayne's voice turned ugly.

"What?"

"You heard me, old man. Money." He pronounced the word slowly.

"It's Wayne, isn't it?" Mr. Tiptop's face changed: his eyes narrowed, and the lines around his mouth turned down. "And there's someone else . . ."

"Get the *money*!" Wayne looked scared. Earl hadn't expected Mr. Tiptop to recognize his voice.

"My check's no good to you," the old man said patiently.

"Go get it." Wayne shoved him, to show he meant business. Mr. Tiptop tripped and caught himself against the wall. "Hurry up," Wayne said. There were dark rings of sweat under the armholes of his shirt. He moved closer to Earl and whispered, "He knows who we are."

Earl nodded.

"It's in the bedroom, in my desk," Mr. Tiptop said. He touched the wall until he came to the bedroom door, then disappeared into the dark.

"We're screwed," Wayne said. "He knows my voice." He looked around. There were two canes leaning by the front door: one white, the other dark. He picked up the second one and flexed it. Sweat beaded on his forehead. "Man, oh man," he said to Earl.

"You said nobody would get hurt!"

"I told you, man, it's all a big mistake."

"I'm leaving." Earl was shaking all over. He put his hand on the door, turned back. Wayne had moved outside the bedroom. "Bring me the check," he called.

The moment stretched, like it was forever. Earl wanted to leave, but he couldn't. Everything was close up now: the dark, the smells, the fear. He held his breath, let it out. "You can't hurt him," he said, loudly.

"Shut up!" Wayne gave him a look that said Earl could be next.

"You can't," Earl said. "I'll turn you in."

"You say anything, I'll cut you into little pieces!"

"I WILL!" Earl couldn't believe that he was shouting.

"COME OUT HERE!" Wayne yelled. The cane was raised.

There was no answer.

Wayne flung open the bedroom door. He went into the darkness, cursing. There was a crash, and someone screamed.

TWENTY-FOUR

What Maynard remembered later was the blood: the blood and Wayne's eyes and the old man moaning.

He heard the shouting through the basement window: "You say anything, I'll cut you into little pieces!" And then "I WILL!" The second voice sounded like a kid.

Maynard stood still, breathed deep. Who could he ask for help? In the whole neighborhood, except for Angela, there wasn't a single soul he knew.

There were more screams, and someone cried out, "Help!" He put his hand on the doorknob, looked around. The street and sidewalk were empty. He took another deep breath and pushed open the door.

The crowded room was dark, but near the back he saw a red-haired boy about his size who saw *him*, too, and rushed forward. The boy grabbed Maynard's arm.

"Help me—Wayne's in there with Mr. Tiptop, beating him up! I can't stop him by myself." He pointed to a door in the far wall.

"Should we call the police?" There was a phone on the table by the piano.

"There's no time! Come quick!"

But by the time they got inside that room the screams had stopped. It was so dark Maynard could hardly see. He found a light switch, flipped it: nothing. There was another one, inside the door, and when he turned that on, a bare, dusty bulb lit the space around the bed. The red-haired boy was kneeling by the body of an old man. "He's hurt all right," he said. "His head's smashed—look here."

Maynard saw the pool of red on the floor, saw the blood gushing onto the boy's hand. He'd watched his dad at the hospital, so he knew what to do. "We've got to stop that bleeding. Here—" He pulled a pillowcase off the bed and quickly folded it. "Press that against the spot while I call an ambulance."

"Wait!" The other boy pointed. In the shadows, by the wall, lay another body. "We got to tie Wayne up. If we don't, he'll kill us both."

Maynard sucked in air. "Where's rope?"

"I don't know. You come hold this, and I'll look for it."

The boy scrambled away, leaving the bloody rag on the floor. Maynard picked it up. Out of the corner of his eye he saw that Wayne was starting to move, stirring as if he'd just waked up. Mr. Tiptop moaned, a high thin sound. "We got to get him to the hospital, Frankie."

The other boy didn't stop moving. "I'm Earl," he called.

Earl disappeared into a room off to the right. From where he crouched by Mr. Tiptop, Maynard could see tools hanging on a pegboard there, and a work counter. When Earl came back he held two lengths of cord. He grabbed Wayne's hands and pulled them behind his back. "Here—help me get it tight."

Reluctantly Maynard left Mr. Tiptop and came forward. Wayne was turning his head slowly back and forth, like a snake getting ready to strike. Earl had Maynard hold the wrists while he looped the rope twice around, pulled the knots taut. "There—we got to do his ankles, too. Take his shoes off first."

They each untied a heavy black shoe, tossed it aside. The smell of dirty socks made Maynard choke. His thoughts were in slow motion: *Strange, with all this blood, to gag at socks* . . . "Here—pull tight now." Earl tested the knots. "Okay, I'll call the ambulance." He went into the front room.

Then Maynard was alone with both of them. The pillowcase he'd used on Mr. Tiptop's head was soaked with blood. He pulled off his T-shirt, wadded it up, and pressed it against the wound. Wayne spoke. His words slurred together: "He *hit* me."

Maynard spotted a hammer lying just beyond Wayne's head, as if someone had done a chore, dropped it there, and forgotten to put it away. Wayne groaned. "Frankie *hit* me," he said.

"F-F-Frankie?" Maynard was so scared he had to push the word out of his mouth.

"He was hiding in the workshop."

"Wh-where'd he go?" But Maynard saw suddenly that the shop had a door onto the street, and it was open.

"Cut me loose," Wayne said. Maynard kept his eyes on Mr. Tiptop's chest. He'd seen his father count breaths, in the hospital; that was something they always wanted to know: *Five, six* . . .

"I can bust these knots if I have to." Wayne was louder now. "I got a knife in my pocket—right here, see? If you don't help me, I'll do it myself."

The hammer was lying there. I should pick it up and hit him, Maynard thought. But he couldn't make himself. When he tried he thought of his father's hands: stitching people together, protecting life.

"W-w-wait," he stammered.

"For what?"

"I'll get you some ice, in a minute."

"ICE?"

"For your head."

He kept watching Wayne. Wayne's hands were just above the pocket. It looked like that was as far as they could reach.

"GET OVER HERE!" Wayne shrieked. From outside there were sirens, and people yelling. Then a policeman ran in, his gun drawn. Maynard almost fainted. "Don't shoot!" he yelped. He could hardly hear himself, with all the noise.

"Here—over here." The policeman pointed to Mr. Tiptop. A pair of medics bent over him. Then the officer turned to Maynard.

"You okay?"

He nodded. The policeman pulled Wayne to his feet, pushed him forward. "He said he has a knife in his pocket," Maynard blurted.

"Thanks."

Wayne looked back. His eyes were dark with rage. "I'm gonna find you, boy, whoever you are. I'm gonna find you and pay you back."

"Shut up!" The policeman shoved him forward, through the door. By then the medics had Mr. Tiptop on a stretcher. They rushed him out without speaking.

So Maynard was alone. He started shaking, as if he had the flu. He could smell blood. Wayne's shoes were still there, lying at odd angles by the bed frame and the wall.

He thought of Frankie again, and looked under the bed, in the closet, and in the workshop. He pulled the door shut there and turned the lock. He went back through the bedroom and looked out. Earl was sitting on the couch, talking to an officer. "He's the one who helped," he said, nodding toward Maynard.

"What were you doing here?" the policeman asked.

"I was looking for his brother. Then I heard screams."

Earl looked surprised. "Frankie's home."

"He isn't either." Maynard shook his head. "Angela thought he'd come here, and she was right, 'cause Wayne said Frankie hit him. I think he was hiding in the workshop. He saw what happened, got a hammer, and crept up behind Wayne. After he hit him, he got scared and left."

"Why didn't we see him?" Earl asked.

"He went back through the workshop. He must have unlocked that door and run outside."

"Speaking of outside, there's someone waiting for *you* there," the policeman said. "We told him you're okay, but he's pretty upset. Your name *is* Maynard, isn't it?"

He went to the front door then. There was a crowd gathered beyond the line of yellow tape, and right in front was his father. He was holding Maynard's blood-soaked T-shirt in his hands. Tears were rolling down his face.

"Dad, I'm here! I'm all right!"

Dr. Glenn couldn't speak. He just clutched Maynard to him, and Maynard let himself go limp, and was carried toward the car like a little child.

TWENTY-FIVE

Angela sat on the front steps. It had been another long day, but better than the one before. Maynard and Addie had visited; and Maynard's dad, too; and then there'd been an accident at Mr. Tiptop's. Angela hadn't seen anything because she'd been told to wait in the car with Addie and not get out, no matter what; but when Maynard and his dad came back, Maynard's shirt was gone, and they looked like they'd been crying.

And Frankie hadn't come home, or Earl either; so Dr. Glenn had taken Angela with him. They'd gone to Addie's house, and then their own, where they had rested, and changed their clothes. Then they'd gone to McDonald's, just for Angela. They'd bought her everything she wanted: a Happy Meal with a strawberry shake and three apple pies. Maynard didn't feel like eating; he just sipped some Coke, to settle his stomach. Angela told him stories about her TV show, which she called *Angela's Great Adventure*. On the program she wore a golden crown and rode an elephant. She went into a cave full of jewels and captured six thieves. When they begged for mercy, she cut their heads off and threw them out the cave door. Dr. Glenn looked like he was going to choke on his chicken sandwich then; but Maynard perked right up. "It's only a *story*," he told his dad, and he laughed out loud.

After that they drove downtown and picked up Mrs. Duke. She said she was a social worker who was going to stay with Angela and Earl and Frankie till they took the bus on Saturday. Her face reminded Angela of the ripe purple plums Daddy used to buy at Central Market, and her smile was easy, like she was used to kids and liked them. Angela wasn't sure she liked her, though; so just in case, she stuck her tongue out. Mrs. Duke laughed. She got a kitchen chair and set it in the doorway of Lula's house, so she could be near Angela on the front steps. They said good-bye to Maynard and his dad.

Then Earl came home in a police car. That was almost the most exciting thing that ever happened, except that Earl didn't seem to feel that way. He looked upset. When Angela asked where he'd been, all he said was, "Shut up."

But later he felt better. Mrs. Duke made an early supper: fried chicken and mashed potatoes and green beans. She called the hospital to check on Mr. Tiptop. The nurses said he was going to have to stay a while—maybe a real long time. "What was the accident?" Angela asked.

"Wayne beat him up."

"Beat up Mr. Tiptop?" Angela had to think about that. "And now he's going to jail?"

"Maybe."

"But you're not . . ." For a second she looked worried. "Are you, Earl?"

"No, the police brought me back here. Told me to stay away from Wayne. I have to pay some people back for what I . . ." He stopped, turned red.

"You didn't hurt Mr. Tiptop, did you, Earl?"

"No."

Angela noticed suddenly that his eyes had changed; there were feelings in them instead of a blank wall. She stared at him close-up, to make sure that it was true. To her amazement she saw what looked like tears. She wondered what in the world would make Earl cry. She didn't ask, though; instead she thought of something that would cheer him up.

"Daddy got a house on the Eastern Shore—we're going there this Saturday on the bus. It has a yard with lots of grass, and a swing out front. Beth-ann's going to live there too."

Earl shook his head, like he didn't believe her; but she insisted: "I've got the picture, and the letter too. It was under Frankie's pillow."

Then Earl found out about the tenant house, and the bus trip, and the missing check. "But your dad is sending money by Western Union," Mrs. Duke said. "I called him a while ago. He's going to talk to all of you tonight."

"We don't have a telephone."

Mrs. Duke pulled a piece of dark plastic out of her pocketbook. She unfolded it once, then again, and held it up for Angela to see. There was a row of tiny buttons, and holes where you spoke in and listened. "Oh!" Angela folded it, unfolded it, played with the buttons. "I want to talk to him right now," she said.

"He's going to wait till Frankie's home."

"How will he know?"

"I'll leave a message at the farm."

"What if Frankie doesn't come?" Earl asked. "What then?"

"You're worried about him, aren't you, Earl?"

Earl imagined Frankie's white face, pictured him hiding in the workshop. He wanted to tell him what had happened in the living room at Mr. Tiptop's. Did he know that Earl had tried to stop the robbery?

Angela looked out the front door. "It's getting dark," she said. "Why hasn't he come home?"

Mrs. Duke stayed calm. She made them each hot milk with honey, and put clean sheets on the beds in the basement room. Earl stood by the window. "I don't want to go to bed until he's here."

"Do you have any idea where he might have gone?" The social worker's face was kind.

Earl shook his head, but Angela nodded. "Maynard said he had a rabbit—he'd been hiding it in the coal box. I think he took it someplace where there's lots of grass—Mexico maybe, or Japan."

Earl stared at her. "How could he hide a rabbit? I mean, we were here all that time and I never saw a rab—" He frowned. "How do *you* know Maynard, anyway?"

"I told you, he's the one with the be-puter! And he's got a scooter too, and he came this morning with his friend, and we looked for the rabbit, but Frankie was already gone. So I sent him to Mr. Tiptop's. And later his dad took us to McDonald's."

"Angela . . ." Earl sighed and turned away, but Mrs. Duke nodded.

"Dr. Glenn is Maynard's father. He called our office last week, asking us to try to find you. Angela must have told him that your aunt had left."

"I did, and I wished on the magic wand to go to McDonald's, only it didn't work until today! Earl, I had a Happy Meal, and a strawberry shake, and all the apple pies I wanted."

But Earl was thinking back, way back, to the day they'd stolen the bikes, and Frankie was sitting on the curb with the rabbit hidden in the sweatshirt. Could he have kept it all this time?

"Frankie had a secret," Angela said. "Didn't he, Earl?"

TWENTY-SIX

Addie lay in bed in her striped pajamas. Her head rested solidly on her pillow, but her mind whirled like leaves tumbling through a windstorm. She'd seen a photograph of Frankie with his family: a chubby, pale boy with short-cropped hair and blue eyes. He wasn't cute, like Angela; nor did he have Earl's smart, thin, wary face. He just stood there, staring out, with nothing unusual about him. Addie could have passed him on the street a thousand times and never looked back. But Angela had said, "*Rabbits* are his favorites." Gazing at her ceiling, Addie thought, We have something in common, after all.

He'd tried to take care of Flag; he must have, or she wouldn't have been there in the coal bin, to drink the water in the overturned cup. She'd have starved, or wilted in the summer heat and died, or been chased and killed by dogs. Addie knew she couldn't have been in that grimy crate the whole time; he must have kept her, somehow, under the bed: the cement floor there was cool, even in this morning's heat. He'd used perfume to cover up the smell. But then Angela had heard something, so he had to change the hiding place.

"Time to turn your light out, honey." Mr. Johnson appeared in the doorway. He hesitated for a minute, then came in and settled his lanky frame on the foot of the bed. He looked at Addie as if she was someone different from the daughter he had known. His eyes were puzzled and a little hurt.

"I've been thinking about what you said—that you weren't sorry for going with Maynard. I was upset and angry at the time, because you lied, and you could have been hurt . . ." His voice caught in his throat. "But later I realized that the two of you did something important: you found the little girl. Now she and her brothers will be cared for. And we know where Flag was, and that she was alive this morning."

He put his hand on top of Addie's. "We'll talk more, okay?"

She nodded. He went out, closing the door softly behind him.

. . .

She couldn't sleep. Each time she shut her eyes images rose up, like flowers opening on a tangle of fast-growing vines: Angela's dirty face; the reek of perfume in that basement room; Maynard's worn-out look when he came back to the car. He wouldn't say what happened at Mr. Tiptop's, only that Frankie wasn't there, and no one died, and things were changed. She didn't have the chance to ask him why, but she saw blood on his hands. She sighed. The rank smell of the trashcan in the rowhouse kitchen came back to her; empty beer cans in a paper bag; the careful arrangement of items on the cupboard shelf—macaroni, ketchup, spaghetti—as if someone had tried to create order where there was none.

She slept for a while then, waking once to the smell of Dr. Glenn's roses wafting through the open window. The church bells at St. James rang out the hour: midnight, Addie thought. She'd heard eleven long ago. Moonlight glowed faintly on the wall. She turned over, bunched her pillow with one hand. She sighed, wriggled her toes, humped her back. She tried to think calm thoughts: waves breaking on a lonely beach, a sunrise, twittering birds. Like roads leading to the same city, every thought came back to Flag.

Addie gave up then. She got out of bed, went downstairs, and drank a glass of juice. The clock on the microwave blinked on and off, casting a ghostly shadow on the countertop. Addie switched on the kitchen TV, turned it off, wandered into the dining room. Her hands touched the table, the sideboard, her father's chair. They had been here, in this room, her whole life: heavy, reliable, unchanging. She sighed. Her feet barely made a sound as she climbed the stairs and went back to her room.

She stood in the window just a minute. The moon had risen over the treetops in her yard; the rabbit hutch was splashed with its pale light. In the background, the hedge loomed dark and solid. She could barely see the house next door. She wondered if Maynard was awake too.

It was then—while she was thinking about Maynard, and how brave he'd turned out to be—that she saw the shadow. It wasn't a shadow, really, she corrected herself; more like a little patch of dark and light that seemed to move, just once, as if the wind had shaken it. But there was no wind on this still night, so she looked again, in the same place by the hedge. Where had it been? There, where a speck of white shone through the thick, dark branches; she put her finger on the window to mark the place. It was moving, she saw suddenly, sliding ever so slowly toward the gap where the footprints had been. She held her breath. If only Maynard were here to see it too, then she'd know she wasn't fooling herself.

But there was something. It was in the gap now, moving slowly forward. Addie leaned against the frame of the window, let her head rest there. She saw that the white was a T-shirt, with a little boy inside. It was coming closer, across the yard.

It was when he stepped into the moonlight that she knew. "Frankie," she murmured; and her hands clenched. He was holding something against his chest. Should she run to the phone, call the police? Should she shout for him to stop? Instead she just stood there holding her breath, afraid that if she blinked he'd disappear.

But he didn't disappear. He came on, steadily, slowly, until he reached the rabbit hutch. She could see the zigzag patterns on his shoes, she even heard the low, rusty creak of the cage door when he swung it open. He stopped then, and took the object he was holding from his shirt and leaned over, so his face rested against it. Addie could feel a scream way in the back of her throat; but she held it down. He bent slowly, lovingly, and placed something in the hutch. The door clicked shut. Addie pounded on the window. He looked up, just for a split second. Then he ran.

She ran, too, thudding down the stairs, out the back door into the yard. He was gone, of course, but she ran to the cage and flung open the latch. The rabbit leaped into her arms. Addie stood there in the dark, holding her.

TWENTY-SEVEN

Earl was the only one who heard the strange sound in the basement room. Mrs. Duke was asleep upstairs, and Angela was curled up on her mattress, the sheet pulled over her head. He got up, went to the basement door, and peered through. In the spring there had been rats in the wall behind the dry sink; Lula had set traps for them, and thrown their bodies in the garbage can outside. Earl wondered if they'd come back. He put one hand in front of him; it was so dark he couldn't even see it. Then he remembered the light in the stairwell. He turned it on and stepped into the doorway.

"Is someone there?"

There was no answer.

"Frankie?" Earl edged forward. Once Frankie had told him there was another way into the house, through the basement, but Earl hadn't paid attention to what he'd said.

He groped forward. The cast-iron furnace rose like a black misshapen monster to his right; on the other side was the sink, and beyond it, the coal bin. A trickle of light from the alley filtered through the grating there. Earl moved toward it. Then, as his eyes got used to the shadows, a shape appeared, sprawled across the lid of the wooden box. When he came near, he saw it was his brother. Frankie's face was streaked with dirt and tears. Earl came up close and touched his arm.

"Are you all right?"

Frankie's eyes opened slowly, and he raised his head. "I didn't let her go the way you told me to," he murmured. "She was so soft, Earl. I liked the way she felt."

"You shouldn't have run away, Frankie. You scared us half to death."

"I took her back. I had to look a long time till I found the yard. This time there was a girl in the house, looking through the upstairs window."

"She was here today, with her friend. They figured out you had the rabbit."

He nodded. "I took care of her all by myself. I didn't tell you or Angela or Mr. Tiptop, 'cause I knew you'd say to take her back."

"She wasn't yours. Those bikes, even the rabbit were *stolen*, Frankie. We told you different, but they were."

"I figured it out." Frankie started crying. Earl waited. After a while he reached over and put his arm around Frankie, but Frankie pushed it away. He sobbed, "You're mean. You were mean to Angela and me."

"I'm sorry."

"And Mr. Tiptop."

"I never wanted to hurt him," Earl said. "I tried to make Wayne stop."

"He banged Mr. Tiptop's head against the radiator. That made me mad. My stubborns came up then."

"You hit him with a hammer—that could have killed him, Frankie."

"You're bad, too," Frankie said angrily. "When Mr. Tiptop came that night, you wouldn't even open the door."

Earl just stood there.

Frankie said, "You're just like Wayne."

Frankie cried and cried. Earl wanted to run away, but he made himself stay. When he was little, he'd been afraid of garbage trucks; when they drove near, Daddy would stand beside him, holding his hand. Earl pretended someone strong was with them now. He put his arm out, but Frankie pushed it away. After a long time Frankie quieted down. Earl got a clean rag and wet it at the dry sink, and helped him wash his face.

"Is that better?" he asked.

"No," Frankie said.

"Do you want something to drink?"

"No."

But there was a mason jar on the window ledge and Earl rinsed it out and filled it with cold water, and Frankie drank.

Earl said, "There's a woman upstairs who's taking care of us until we go on Saturday. And the police have Wayne—a boy named Maynard helped me tie him up. And the police are after Lula, too, for leaving us. And Mr. Tiptop's in the hospital . . ."

"Where are we going?" Frankie asked.

"Daddy got a house on the Eastern Shore. Beth-ann's going to move in too."

Frankie said, "I'm not going anywhere with you."

Even in the dark Earl could see the stubborn set of his shoulders, and his jaw, so he didn't argue.

Later Frankie went into the bedroom. He was so tired and hurt that Earl had to help him walk. When they passed the stairwell, Earl saw that his knees were bleeding. Frankie said he'd banged into a stone wall when he was running in the dark, trying to get home. Earl washed his knees with the wet rag, peeled off his filthy shirt. He pulled back the clean sheets on the bed, and tucked Frankie in. "Good night," he said.

Frankie wouldn't answer.

But later, after they'd both slept a little while, Frankie woke him up. He whispered, "You know what, Earl?"

"What?"

"I wonder if she had another name all that time."

"You mean the rabbit?"

He nodded.

"I don't know," Earl said. He could hardly keep his eyes open. "No one told me."

"If she did, I don't mind," Frankie said. "But I gave her a name while she was here. I'm the only one that knows it, besides her. I thought it up all on my own."

"What was it?" Earl asked.

"It's secret," Frankie said, but a minute later he whispered, "Promise you won't tell?"

"I won't," Earl said.

"Angela would."

"I'm not Angela."

Frankie said, "Her name was Spot."

EPILOGUE

Mrs. Duke put them on the Greyhound bus.

When they talked on the phone, Daddy decided to come and get them Saturday in Beth-ann's car, dropping her off at work on his way there. But Angela said she'd been waiting all her life to take a real trip, the kind where you buy a ticket for the plane or train or bus and give it to the conductor when you get on board. And after she fussed and cried, Daddy said the bus would be okay, only to be careful, after all that they'd been through.

And then they were on it: a big silver bus, with its own bathroom and little TV sets fastened to the walls. They sat in the back, so they could have the whole long seat to spread out on. Earl checked the backpack: the sandwiches and juice and cookies were there, and the coloring books, and the map with their route drawn in blue. Mrs. Duke had gone over it with him, so they'd know where to get off: "Here's Easton, and Salisbury, and Pocomoke City, and Oak Hall, and right down here is Tillington." "What if we're asleep?" Earl asked. "Then your dad will come on board and wake you up." She'd smiled reassuringly. "He'll be there, Earl. He can hardly wait to see you."

Then the engine started, and Earl opened the window, and they leaned out and waved good-bye. Mrs. Duke waved, too. The bus backed out, rounded the corner, and pulled away.

"Good-bye!" Angela called out the window. "Good-bye, Howard Street! Good-bye, Park Avenue! Good-bye, Orleans Street!"

Then she started in on other things, and for the first time since he'd come home that night Frankie seemed to cheer up too. He called: "Good-bye, church! Good-bye, park! Good-bye, school!" Angela thought of people: "Good-bye, Aunt Lula! Good-bye, Mr. Tiptop! Good-bye, Maynard!"

Maynard had come to visit yesterday. This time his dad brought him, in the car. Maynard and Angela sat on the front steps talking. Maynard looked the same, but he seemed nervous. He said he was in major trouble for going places he wasn't allowed to, and lying about it. For the rest of the summer he'd have to stay

224 ·

at the hospital daycamp with a bunch of little kids because he couldn't be trusted on his own. "But I don't
care," he said. "I've had enough adventures for at least
a month. I'm ready to read a book, or watch TV."

"You can watch my show," Angela said.

"And in the fall, the Johnsons plan to get new
bikes. When they do, Dad's going with them to get
bikes for him and me. Then we can ride together!
Maybe we'll ride all the way downtown, to the harbor!" The thought of fat Dr. Glenn riding a bike made
Maynard smile, and Angela laugh out loud.

"Maybe you can ride all the way to the Eastern
Shore," Angela said. "Then me and you can get married."

"I don't know about that." Maynard had been
thinking, if he had to pick a girl to care about, it
would be Addie. The morning after Flag came home
she'd kissed him on the cheek. He touched the spot
her lips had touched.

"You're coming to visit me, aren't you?"

"Maybe. If Wayne's not anywhere around." Maynard stopped then. "I'm scared of Wayne," he said.

"Wayne stinks! But Daddy says he'll go to jail for
what he did."

"He might get out, though."

"If he does, he better stay away from us. And if he asks your name, I'll tell him I don't know." Angela stuck her tongue out. "That's for him," she said.

Before he left, Maynard copied down her new address in his notebook—"So we can write, and send each other stories." And he handed her an envelope. "Addie sent this—give it to Frankie, okay?"

"I won't forget," Angela said.

But all that day and the next morning they'd been busy. Mrs. Duke washed everything and held it up to them, to see if it still fit. They'd packed the checkers set and Frankie's marbles; the pictures they'd brought with them from Beth-ann's; some comic books and crayons. Earl collected Daddy's letters, fastening them together with a rubber band. Mrs. Duke helped them write to Mr. Tiptop. They said they wished that they could see him; but the hospital wouldn't let them in his room till they were twelve. "I'll be married then," Angela said in her part of the letter. "I'm going to marry the boy with the be-puter in his room."

Saturday morning they dressed in their best clothes. Mrs. Duke braided Angela's hair into two short pigtails and tied the ends with ribbons. Now she checked, to be sure the ribbons were still there.

"Look!" Earl pointed out the window. The bus was gaining speed, passing lines of rowhouses, and shut-down and working factories, and the harbor, with its sailboats and tugboats and barges. They rode past new hotels and the baseball stadium, its bright pennants drooping in the summer heat. A ramp led to the interstate. Then Earl could turn and see the city skyline: office buildings, banks, apartments. The highway unrolling behind him seemed like his own life, unwinding like string off a spindle, because everything he'd known, good or bad, was tied to the city.

"I spilled my juice!" Angela cried. There was a purple splotch on the seat. Earl mopped at it with a wad of paper napkins. Then Frankie finished his drink and wanted Earl's too.

"No way." But he couldn't forget how glad he'd been to see Frankie, the other night. "You can have half," he said. Frankie smiled like Earl had given him a piece of gold.

They crossed a bridge, a long gray span that seemed to stretch for miles over the choppy water. "That's the bay," Earl said. "Mrs. Duke showed me, on the map. The other side's the Eastern Shore."

They clapped where the bridge touched down, though it still didn't seem like country: just houses and stores and highway. But later they saw cows in a meadow—real live cows. Earl had seen them in the children's zoo, but he'd forgotten how big they were. Frankie's nose was pressed against the window. Angela claimed she'd seen much bigger cows, on a trip out west, but Earl told Frankie she was lying.

Just past Easton, a woman three seats up began to talk to them. She seemed friendly at first but soon she started asking questions: "Where are you from? Who's your father? Why didn't he take you with him in the first place?" Earl tried to explain, but it came out sounding like Daddy didn't care. The woman, who had a red nose and squinty eyes, seemed to think she'd have done better. "When Carrie was in camp, I wrote to her every day, to make sure she was all right," she said.

She got off in Cambridge, wishing them well before she left. Angela refused to say good-bye. She rooted in the backpack and pulled out the broken yardstick.

"I'm putting a spell on her."

"Angela . . ." Earl didn't want any trouble. "Put that away!"

She made a face but did as she was told.

Later they had ham sandwiches and chips and Oreo cookies. The juice was gone, but there was a bottle of water to share: special water, with pine trees and a lake on the green label. Frankie got nervous suddenly, and started asking questions: Why would someone sell water? Would he go to school on the Eastern Shore? Would there be music in first grade?

"I don't know," Earl said.

"Is Mr. Tiptop better now?"

Earl didn't like to think about the old man lying in bed in the hospital. "I don't know," he said.

Then Angela remembered the envelope. She dug in her pocket, pulled it out, and gave it to Frankie. He didn't understand who it was from.

"Addie," Angela said. "The girl with yellow hair. She came looking for her rabbit."

Frankie opened it and looked inside. There was a picture of Spot, staring right at him, as if she knew that he was there. He put his fingers on the glossy paper, stroked her head.

"I'll keep this forever," he told Angela.

"Maybe you'll get a real pet—a puppy, or a kitty."

But Frankie shook his head.

"You could get another rabbit," Angela said. "A brown one, like her." Frankie smiled then, like *that* was a good idea.

.   .   .

Later Earl turned from the window. "Look—that's corn! A whole field of corn. And over there's pumpkins!"

"What's that smell?" Angela held her nose. They passed a group of long, low sheds that stunk like poop. Earl tried to close the window, but by the time he got it up the smell was gone. "Chicken farms," somebody else muttered. A river flowed by, slow and dark, curving through a forest of tall trees.

Then Frankie fell asleep. Angela stuck the backpack under her head like a pillow and lay across the seat. Earl kept looking out the window. Pink sky edged the land beside the road near Pocomoke. An old man shuffled off the bus there, carrying two plastic bags. From the platform he saw Earl watching and smiled. Where was he going? Earl asked himself. Was there an old woman, too, in a shabby, crooked house, waiting for him to come home?

Someone was waiting for *him*. Earl knew he'd made mistakes: stolen things, let one man get robbed and Mr. Tiptop get hurt bad. On the phone Daddy said they'd have to find a way to make things right. His voice had sounded sad. "We're family," he said just before they hung up. "That's what you have in the end; not money, not things, but people." When he said it, it sounded right; but later Earl was angry. When he and Frankie and Angela tried to keep things going, where had Daddy been? Hadn't he known Lula was irresponsible? Wasn't there a way he could have checked on them?

He sat still. Through the window he saw a chunk of moon, rising faintly in the blue-gray sky. Lights flickered in the houses, pale at first, then stronger as the night came on. Fireflies brushed against the windows of the bus. Were they brushing against the windows of the new house, too, flickering in the dark backyard? Would he and Angela and Frankie catch them in a jar? When it was bedtime, would they open it and let them go? Earl closed his eyes and leaned back in his seat. After a while he fell asleep.

Angela saw him. She'd been watching out of half-closed eyes, waiting for him to doze off so she could do whatever she wanted. Now she bounced on the seat of the bus. She took off her shoes and rubbed her feet on the velvety cushions. She ate five Oreos and sucked the crumbs off her fingers. She looked into the backpack for something else to do. The wand was there, where Earl had made her put it. She checked to make sure he was really asleep. Then she took it out. "What shall I wish for?" she asked herself.

It was a funny problem. Before she'd wished for Daddy and Beth-ann, but she was about to see them. They'd wanted a house, but now they had one, and mean Wayne was left behind in the city, with a bruise on his head. She glanced at Frankie; he was sleeping with the rabbit's picture clutched against his chest. He'd probably have his own pet soon. Angela moved up a seat, to be alone and think. That was when she saw.

There was another child, looking in the window. Angela was shocked and a little scared; she stuck her tongue out, in case the other child was mean, but that girl or boy—she wasn't sure which—did it, too. She looked to see if the child was brown-skinned, like Maynard; if his hair was long or short. For a minute she thought she saw Addie's braids; but when she moved close to the glass the face staring in at her was wider and pale, like Frankie's. She gave a wary glance and thought she recognized Earl's sharp eyes, glancing back. But when she checked the seat behind her, Earl and Frankie were asleep. She stopped, looked forward, then quickly turned. The child was still there. This time she looked like someone Angela never met, but nice. Angela laughed. The other one laughed, too.

Then she knew what she was meant to do. She held the wand in her lap and made a wish: not for herself, because she was happy, but for the other one. She wished for all the things she'd already got: a house, and people who loved her, a backpack filled with food, a trip to wonderful and distant lands. "May you have adventures, and stories to tell, and good luck every day," she whispered; and in the darkness, the other child smiled and whispered, too.